4D

a psychonovel

MAJA D'AOUST

Cover by Maja D'Aoust and Suzanne Uchytil
Interior design by Suzanne Uchytil (linktr.ee/suzanneuchytil)

ISBN 979-8-218-17286-2

www.witchofthedawn.com

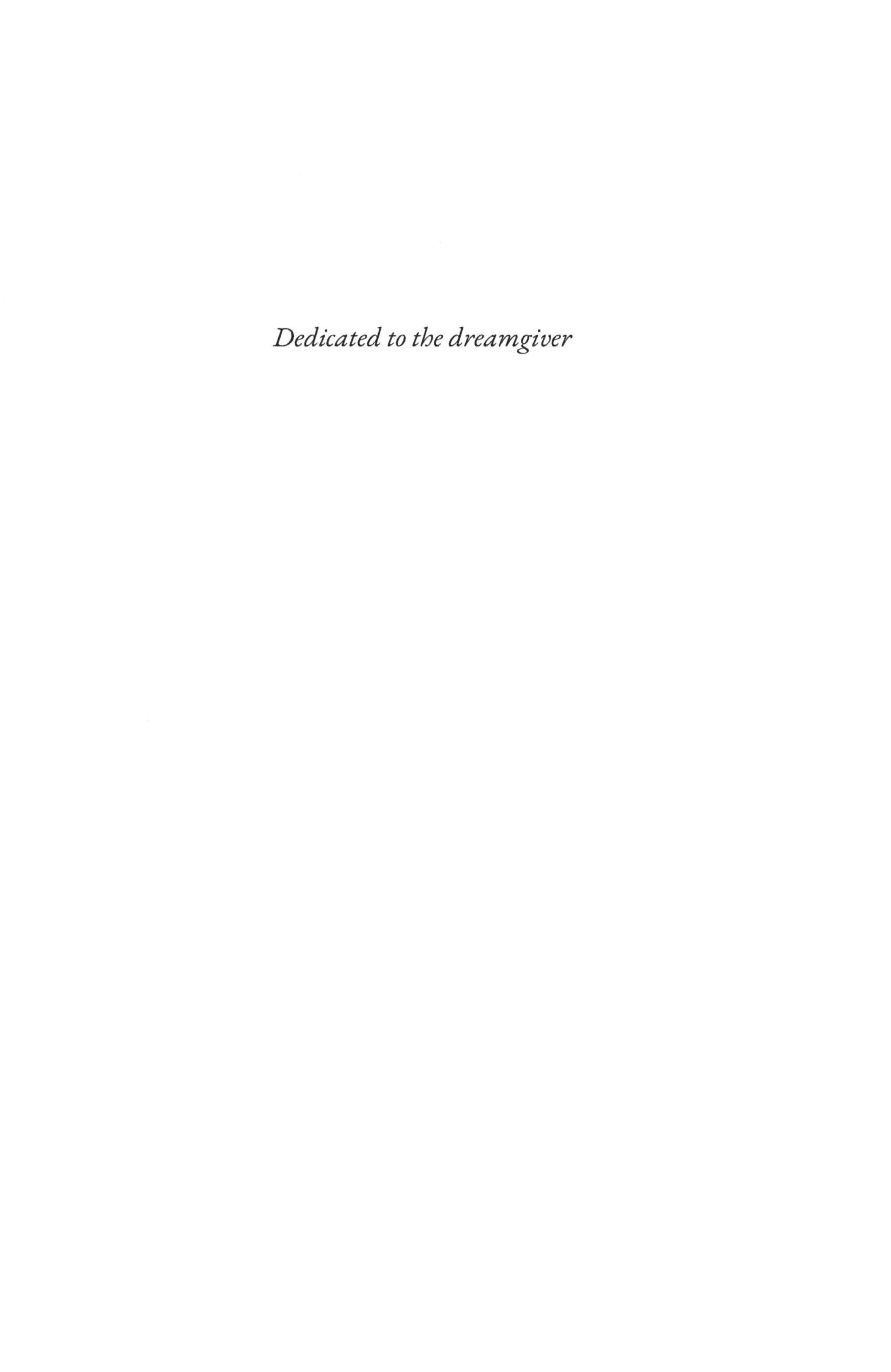

Dedicated to the dreamgiver

Table of Contents

The Portal

Shhh, shhh, shhh. The sound of bicycle tires on the damp street beat out a rhythmic percussion as I rode through the shitty part of town. The horizon was lined with smoke stack trees. The factories were packed in tight cement cubes mimicking mountains. It was my favorite time of day, or daynight, as I called it. The time when the sky was trading shades of midnight blue and neon orange. The colors made no sense, they didn't belong, shouldn't be there together. The atmosphere was clear and the air was crisp after the rain. The Sun had set but it wasn't dark yet. I saw the last gasps of light rays to the right while the moon was rising on the left. Daynight. What a beautiful place this Earth is, I thought to myself as I tarried on into the twilight.

It was the first daynight of work at my new job. Quests for fame and fortune had all landed me here. I traced the timelines over and over, trying to discover the fork in the road that led to this arrival point, but I wasn't able to pick up the scent. There had to be some mathematical equation where I could solve for X and the answer would come forward. My life was a big hunt after some strange beast whose footprints kept changing in some secret code from a Turing machine, indecipherable and purposely misleading. I had fine aspirations, focused on goals. I wasn't some lost ne'er do well floating by on a breeze.

Despite well-aimed ambitions, I was a complete failure. Everything I did felt wrong.

The caustic voice in the back of my head had quite a bit to say about it. I knew intuitively that I was not at "fault" but was unable to convince my internal monologue of this. Some folk call it an "inner critic," I guess the religious call it Satan, whatever that means. Not sure what its name is, but I can testify it exists simply because I have to listen to it all the time and it won't shut up. All day it had been berating failures inside my brain torture chamber, unbeknownst to the rest of the world, a secret, outwardly silent assailant. I always thought of it as a virus or bacteria, some kind of recurring infection, opportunistic upon a lack of wellbeing. Right now, it was riding me harder than I was pedaling this bicycle, that was carrying my sad sorry ass to the strip club to go to work.

Experiencing self-inflicted bullying had its perks, I've never really cared what other people said about me, thanks to my own aggressive dialogue, equivalent to living with a wrestling villain as a roommate. You know, the kind who gets up in your face, spitting, disregarding your boundaries and basically being a total jerk. There was nothing anyone on the outside could say to me that was worse than what I said to myself. An ambush of insults constantly running in loops, amplified during defeat.

Ugh. I guess I should be grateful I can even do this, it could be worse, there is an undeniable silver lining, who am I to complain? I had always been disdainful of self-pity. At least there was something keeping me from utter ruin. I never understood how anyone appraised the actions of another without acknowledging the heartlessness of humanity which drives the individual to unseemly undertakings. The self-righteous gasps, the disbelief, were easily answered if anyone had experienced loss. I had no respect for those willing to look down on someone in a position they themselves had never been in. Yet, I simultaneously judged the titty bar. I wanted to reject those who would evaluate me for being a stripper, but also did not release my judgment of exotic dancers and a dismay at doing the job. Ah the beauty of a paradox.

"Get over yourself, you're just a hypocrite, not a philosopher," whined my nagging mental partner.

"True, true," I said aloud, though there was no one there. Guess I'll do creative facial expressions and act as if I'm glad to be here. Fake it till you make it right? Be here now, or whatever those old men say who want to emotionally manipulate the unfortunate into giving them money. There should be wisdom in there somewhere. I crept up to the back entrance of the club as the stars were making their appearance. A cool breeze brushed my cheek and I set my foot down in the alley.

"The stars are coming out, it must be an omen for your Hollywood debut," mocked mind. I looked down, there were rats everywhere. Glamorous. I couldn't find a spot to leave my bike amidst the piles of trash and vermin extending into the cityscape, so I carried it up the steps and went inside. After some embarrassing struggle with the weighty door, I crashed into the scene. I had definitely quantum leaped into some other dimension through a portal. The stark contrast of going from desolate garbage to this abundant secret city of smut was a testament to compartmentalization. The wave of sound and smells and sights punched me in the face. The shock that this was occurring within the walls of a single space in the middle of the warehouse wasteland that surrounded it was truly wizardry on some level I could not understand, but only bear witness to. The club was already packed, what the Hell?

Dammit. I'm late. The girls were on the make, each one doing their darndest to get attention. Stark bodies were thrust all over the men as I awkwardly tried to wheel my bicycle along in full view of the guests and the already half naked employees. I looked up and wasn't paying attention while I swiftly caught my shoelace in the greasy bike chain, yanking me down in a violent collapse that almost made me puke because my torso caught the seat in the center of my squishy entrails. A huge wall of a man standing in the corner spun his head in my direction, locking in eye contact and frowning profusely. The bouncer. He certainly did bounce his way over to me in a hurry, to ensure he would make my acquaintance, I must have looked quite the mess.

"Excuse me ma'am," he said in an authoritative dad-esque voice that implied I was going to be grounded. "I think you are in the wrong place," grabbing me by my elbow, showing me the way out.

"Oh, I'm so sorry, I'm new here, I wasn't sure where to go, Bobby told me to show up but forgot to tell me where to come in at, my name's Angela," I pleaded in the most sugary, innocent voice I could muster.

"You *work* here?" His eyes nearly crossed. "Hang on, don't move, I'll be right back." He shoved his way through the crowd and disappeared into the dark, leaving me standing there like a total tool with my bicycle. My puffy coat was admittedly pretty dirty, my sneakers were grubby, and I just stood, holding my bike, the house music playing, the lights flashing, and girls rubbing up on the semi-inebriated clientele. Talk about spoiling the suspension of disbelief, what a buzzkill.

"*You're off to a great start there, toots,*" the teasing tone offered from somewhere in the God-knows-where region of my intellect.

"Not now!" I snarked back at it.

"*Rain check?*" it shot at me.

"You look lost in space." I heard a strange man's voice in the corner of my ear and jerked my head as I came back into the unfortunate razor clarity of the surroundings. The man laughed to himself as he bent his head down to light his cigarette. He was leaning up against the wall and raised his left knee up, resting his foot on the crusty bright pink paint. His dark hair had a substantial amount of grease keeping it in place, the place he had obviously placed it carefully in that arrangement, although why I can't say, there is no accounting for taste. He wasn't ugly, but he had a feeling about him. Not everyone has a feeling, or even makes me notice them for that matter. But he had a feeling. He felt like a coyote. Definitely a coyote. I called them the coyote people, the ones who weren't evil, but also weren't good. Coyotes were smart though and got what they wanted, they had a certain way about them.

"Did you get beamed down from bum fuck, babe?" A disconcerting cavalier confidence that made my skin crawl filled his voice.

"Haha maybe I did, it's my first day here." I laughed nervously, as my intestines pulled back into the deep recesses of my abdomen. Why do you get to talk to me? I pondered.

"Oh, you *work* here?" he said, animating the features of his sharp and pointy face.

"Guilty as charged," I replied, trying not to meet his eyes for very long. His gaze canvassed the terrain of my body with the excruciating surveillance intensity of a Goddamn military operation. I felt his nostrils expand as he tried to smell me from where he was casually and motionlessly standing. Fucking coyotes.

He exhaled a huge plume of smoke that drifted directly into my face, and I crinkled my nose. Every time I smelled tobacco, I traveled into the back seat of a Pontiac station wagon in the snowy tundra of winter when my father smoked his cigarettes and rolled the window down in such a tiny crack that the amount of smoke actually leaving the car was a matter of atomic particles. He felt my reaction to his fumes and took another big inhale, unfazed by my displeasure, just watching it. He enjoyed looking at things, a voyeur I surmised. A serpentish sentence crawled from his cracked brittle lips;

"Well sweetheart, I'll be here all night, looking forward to your act, I can't wait to see what you do with that bicycle." His words were slime that oozed over me and there was not a thing I could do about it but stand there and let them, I was a caged animal getting oil poured all over me. Ew.

"Hey, that's why I earn the big bucks mister," I replied half-heartedly, avoiding absorbing any ounce of the shared space between us. I started to walk away, I had no place to go, but I took several steps in some random direction to make it seem I had a destination, within the cramped corridor that led to less than nowhere. "Be here now," I tried to repeat to myself, uselessly clinging to some culturally acceptable spiritual advice that had absolutely no pragmatic value in this moment. "Disassociate now," I laughed in response.

"*Aw, you found your new boyfriend.*" My witty asshole leered at me as my brain tissue pulsed in dismay.

"Shh, here he comes," I retorted. The bouncer was lumbering his way back to me, leading with his face that wore a grumpy scowl. Hilarious, I'm getting flak in the sleaze fest, didn't see that coming. So much for righteous indignation.

"*You worked hard to get to the bottom,*" the incessant imagination replied.

"I said be quiet." I talked to myself so often, I barely noticed it anymore.

"Angela, follow me please we will get you set up." Apparently, I had gotten the A-Okay. Impressive he remembered my name, but I guess he was making sure I was who I said I was. Although I couldn't really imagine a situation where someone would pretend to be a stripper, and that made me stifle a giggle. We made our way through the hall when the bartender came up to us;

"Hey, sorry, someone wants to buy her a drink?" The drink slinger sized me up hesitantly, not sure if the bouncer was escorting me out of the building but obviously wanting to do his job.

"Tell him she can't drink while she is working," the bouncer replied gruffly.

"Sure thing, Gus," he muttered, as he faded back into the disco lights.

"Right this way, Angela," Gus said, motioning me to go through a heavy steel door that he opened in a husky tug.

"Thanks." I gratefully ducked my head down and disappeared into whatever world lay on the other side of that wormhole. It was so dark as I turned the corner that I almost spun back around, but revolted at the idea of asking Gus for any further instructions, so I just kept walking, holding my bicycle. My eyes swiveled in their sockets, wet white fists grasping frantically at what little light remained. I went through another bend and in a flash the lights were so bright I had to squint my gaze into a slit.

"Hi Baby!" The Betty Boop voice poured syrupy into my ears, the environment filled my senses so severely, my hypervigilance kicked into gear. I looked over and saw the semi-naked visage of a 20ish woman holding a glass of champagne, she had dayglow braided hair extensions, a G-string and hot-pink pasties.

"Who let her in here?" A monotone, broken souled creak came from the lower right. I tried not to stare, I would need to make some sort of reply.

"Hi, I'm Angela. It's my first day." I tried to smile.

"Fake it till you make it, be here now," my rapier wit stabbed.

"Oh my God, a virgin!" Sang the sickly-sweet voice again, she popped up out of her seat and laughed at her own joke in a kind of donkey bray.

"Ha, first time that has ever been said in a strip club," seethed the sardonic voice of the reptile woman. Her thin frame was cloaked in a black satin robe and her dark eye make-up nearly extinguished the rest of her face into oblivion.

"You are funny!" I said as I shuffled my feet, looking for somewhere to put my bicycle in the tiny space that was shoved full of skanky outfits and miscellaneous platform boots.

"Is it cool if I stick my bike here?" I asked as I plopped it into the least offensive spot.

"Is that part of your act?" The goth one asked, contemptuously curling her upper lip.

"Wow, not sure what ya'll do around here, but this is how I get to work, haha." The nervous laughter fell flat upon their judgmental glares, a belly flop in a pool.

"Oh shoot, gotta jet. Good luck, fresh bait!" Jeered hair extensions after she picked up her phone and saw the time. The mismatched pair both made haste down the dark corridor to the fray of dollar bill producing barking dogs. Swiftly alone now in the overly lit room that smelled like drug store perfume and douche, I took off my backpack and dug around to pull out the ridiculous "bottom" I had procured and went about getting myself together to do my, er, job. I removed my clothes and suited up, got my hair and face together.

"Thank God for make-up!" Laughed my counterpart, taking every opportunity to dig the knife in. I just rolled my eyes at myself as I looked in the mirror. I tried not to pay much attention as I went into "check out mode" and drifted somewhere far away where a song was playing in the background. "Dissociate now." I appreciated the genius retort to the idiot philosophers who clearly had never been in anything remotely like this position. Staring at my reflection, trying to make sure I got the eyeliner on right, I stopped and peered at the flesh of my facade. Mouth parted, tongue sticking out and one eye open, I applied the thick dark ink to my eyelid.

"Even a clown has to prepare," howled the heckler. I couldn't connect to the face, it seemed so foreign, all lit up. I was putting on paint, but I wasn't able to find the place where I did it on purpose, I didn't feel like myself, I was losing who I was in this godforsaken place. When I figured I appeared presentable-ish, I got up and headed back into the chaotic fray of the club.

My eyes fought against the turbulence of darkness as they tried to drink in some light. I staggered into the long passageway, a naked baby being birthed into some other realm. I popped out the other side to an empty foyer, everyone had disappeared. The previously packed front room was vacant except for Gus and the bartender who nearly dropped their jaws at the sight of me as I came through the heavy door. I had just stepped on to the stage of the most surreal pageant ever, except it was my life. I was Alice entering the Mad Hatter's tea party. The fucking coyote was still seated at the bar, piercing me with his eyes, seemingly frozen in place, looking like he shit himself squinting in exaggerated concentration.

"Go say hi to your boyfriend." The tender poke from my darling psyche.

Before I could even inhale to ask any questions, Gus was flashing across the room in a lightning bolt, eyes wide and mouth pursed into a grimace. He tried to purposefully stand between us, placing his girth in the coyote and the bartender's line of sight.

"Angela, where the fuck is your top?" he whispered aggressively.

"What?" I asked, as if he was speaking in another language.

"Your top. You can't come out here that way," he spat through his gritted teeth.

I glanced down, I was topless wearing less-than panties, and peeked back at him, this had to be a joke.

"Um, this is a strip club, I thought maybe we weren't supposed to wear clothes." Making a face as squishy and sarcastic as possible.

"Jesus Christ, are you for real? That's only on stage when you are performing and you need pasties even then," Gus articulated.

"Ooooh, I'm so sorry, haha silly me. You don't need to get bent out of shape about it, it's not my fault no one told me! How am I supposed to know?!" I justified to the Goliath standing before me.

"Did someone need to call you today to tell you that you need to eat breakfast? You've been to a club before, right?" I blushed and turned red at his observation.

"Oops you're busted, haha," laughed the inner tormentor.

"Well, I said, this is my first day" I replied to Gus, whose eyes gaped as wide as his mouth and he grabbed me by the elbow, leading me back down the hallway.

"Go find yourself some slutty outfit to put over yourself until it's time for you to go on, and put some tape or some shit over your chest for Christ's sake," he grumbled as he shoved me back through the abyss.

"Dammit" I mumbled.

"Wow, fucking up your stripper job, eh," mind mercilessly mentioned.

"Shut up, I have to concentrate!" I yelled out loud, nervously checking around to make sure no one heard me screaming at myself. I quickly ransacked the dilapidated costumes strewn about the room till I found one at the bottom of a heap, hoping any diseases that might have been attached to the person who owned it had been able to live out their life cycle. It was a fucking wonder woman outfit.

"Oh well," I said, smiling. "Any port in a storm." I threw it on and went back out. Gus looked up at me as I came through and quickly covered his face with his hand shaking his head. The bartender gave me a side eye and turned around, avoidantly seeking to busily wash some glasses. The coyote, who had barely moved from where he was, lifted his hands to give an overly exaggerated round of applause, his cigarette dangling precariously from his lips, threatening to drop in his lap at any moment. I threw him a mock curtsy and ran over to Gus, unable to figure out what I needed to do now.

"Hey, by the way, where did everyone go?" I asked, my eyes darting around.

"They are in the main room, through the curtain over there. You're late. Bobby is waiting for you. But uh . . . your outfit. Never mind, you better get going." His face contorted in chagrin as he snorted, annoyed that he even had to talk to me.

"Well, pardon us all to hell that we don't seem to get the common courtesy of a strip club bouncer who seems to feel we don't deserve the time of day. I mean, dude, we showed you our tits, you can at least be polite," protested the pundit. *"Poor baby, you have to talk to a naked woman, you have it so rough. Boohoo for you."* All the judgment for strippers magically washed away at that moment and gave them a full pardon, as though I had just been appointed governor. I turned and headed to the big room, taking a deep gulp of air as though I was about to dive into an ocean.

I gagged uncontrollably from the odor. The smell. How could it stink this way? Were there dead animals under the floors? Everything was pitch black except for the stage lights and it took me a minute before I could even see anything. The panorama came into view, clearer than a scientist examining a slide of gonorrhea under a microscope as I grazed the room with my assaulted eyeballs. The men, if you could call them that, were snakes slithering about or slinking in corners. I could see them, or what was left of them, they had been reduced to some sort of caricature of themselves, a parody of their libidos. The girls were even worse. Hungry faces darting for dollars, chickens pecking for worms. I had walked into the barnyard of a perv farm. Who am I? A chicken? Or a snake? I would never judge a stripper again, it was the world, I blamed the world. Our core animal nature was so present, so visible in everyone here. Who is to hold accountable for lust of any kind? Is a personal character to be faulted for their hunger caused by millions of years of instinct, starvation and needs? I saw the whole situation in its largest scope and it was terrifying. I had been fooled by culture's imposed imagined scapegoating. I understood a lot at that moment. How folks could disdain entire groups of people for example. I really internalized knowledge of prejudice, I got it. This was it. I wasn't sure what to do with myself and felt like a child standing in the corner who had to pee but didn't know where the bathroom was. The urgency to escape was chemically palpable within my body. I couldn't deny or pretend past it. Even if I had the wherewithal to overcome my base drives, there was no silencing this shout to remove myself from the room I had found myself in, I had to listen. I was quite sure my displacement was achingly transparent to whatever state of mind the rest of the crowd was enjoying, and I began having a panic attack as my refusal amassed. I could almost see my anxiety grow into some sort of creature, standing beside me, ready to wreak unknown havoc that I had nothing to do with. I wondered inwardly if this was how it was for the Viking berserkers, inhabited by some animal they had invoked and then left wantonly at its whim.

I hugged the wall for support, it was cool and slimy, devoid of comfort. The beat of my heart drowned out the music blasting while the girls danced. How could my inside be so much louder than their attempts to externally overpower everything? My internal body won the competition for my attention at that moment. I watched, embarrassed, as a man seated in front of me waved over a girl to his table with his mouth askew. He had so little awareness as his entire being was focused outwardly at the things in front of him that he seemed to have lost control over his physical state. I guess that's what they wanted though really, to become lost in the outside, and to abandon the inner world. I was unable to achieve this, and it was noticeable. Damn my self awareness. I was slightly envious of their ability to disregard such situations as I now had to deal with.

"*No,*" said the voice inside my deepest self. Ughhhhhh I heard myself respond. I couldn't do it. I just couldn't. A feeling welled up that was . . . grief? I actually had grief like someone had died, I mean, it smelled as though someone died anyway. Grieving over the state of humanity as it loomed across this particular location of the planet earth, a tear physically escaped onto my cheek to confirm the crystalized realization. Horrified, I spun on my heel in a ballerina maneuver and ran back out the other way.

"Jesus Christ Angela!" I heard Gus exclaim as I brisked past him. "What's your damage now?" I ignored him and ran back to get my clothes through the long hallway.

"*Another suitcase in another hall.*" My incessant mental dialogue was singing the song from *Evita* as I tried to concentrate on getting the fuck out of there as quickly as I could.

"*Where am I going to?*" quietly I said internally. I couldn't see anything. I felt my way with my hand along the damp drippy corridor. My eyes searched for the faintest shred of light. I could barely feel my feet walking on anything. I had the sensation I might be completely floating in midair, the only string tying me to this world was my hand on the slick wall. The black invaded me. My form lost consistency and was unable to keep it out, my skin was torn open by tiny blades of nothing, allowing entrance to the heavy tar of the dark. Finally, a shrapnel of light led me into salvation, and I opened the door. I threw on my clothes and made a dash to get out, praying that no one would talk to me. I totally got why so many magicians would invest in spells of invisibility and wished I had more discipline in that department. If some practice could have afforded me the ability to simply disappear it was more valuable than anything on Earth right now. I emerged back out in the open air outside the club and was relieved to find that Gus must have gotten occupied with something other than me, so I slipped silently into the night. I had barely gotten down the stairs when someone grabbed my arm. My eyes bulged out of their sockets like a goldfish, I was caught completely off guard. I whipped my head around ready to enter assault mode and my intestines sunk to my toes. It was the coyote. Shit.

"Your boyfriend," mind cooed at me. *"Give him a kiss,"* it hissed.

The Ride

L et go of me!" I shouted with as much threat as I could muster, trying to sound tough but losing my breath, revealing my fear. He instantly dropped his grip and held up his hands in surrender.

"Sorry, sorry, relax. I'm not going to hurt you, I just noticed you were leaving in a hurry and wanted to see if you were ok." My mouth gaped open in shock and disbelief at his sincerity.

"Good lookin' out, but I have to go."

"Where are you gonna go? You need a ride?" Damn. I didn't have anywhere to go. I got evicted which is what prompted me to take this fucking job in the first place. My stuff was all sitting in storage.

"*Where am I going to?*" Shut up brain, you are not helping me right now.

"*So what happens now?*" Ugh.

"I, I don't know," I answered him reluctantly. He took out a cigarette and motioned the pack towards me offering me one.

"No thanks" I said. The flint sparked and the flame rose from his lighter as he drew it in towards his cigarette, the flash of the fire lit up his skin, covered in deep pores. He looked at me for a while.

"You don't belong here, I get it. I got a nose for people. Something is off with you. Say, why don't you just get a room and figure out what you are doing, my treat." I froze in place. This is it, this must be how women get murdered by bad guys. This is where I go to the second location Oprah talked about. Is life really this cliché? I checked around expecting to see a control room somewhere or people behind a two-way mirror.

"Don't worry, nothing creepy, you just need to catch a break is all. You can have the room all to yourself, no strings attached." My stomach was a muddy, rainy day with a slug slithering through it. My chest contracted. I had been counting on whatever money I made tonight to pay for a place to crash. It's so unfair. This is how it goes down, this is why people don't make it in life, by being forced into situations such as this. It wasn't fair that I couldn't pay rent either. It wasn't fair that I lost my other job because I ratted out the guy who stabbed me in the back. Nothing was fair, I didn't want this. I didn't choose this. The panic rose in my chest at my total lack of control. All those people who talk about how your attitude can shape your life are full of shit. I did nothing to deserve this. Tony Robbins was a liar. We are nothing but puppets being driven along by some esoteric pull of the strings of fate. The illusion of co-creation is a joke. Nothing I did could have possibly landed me here. My crystal ball never showed me this. I didn't deserve this.

"**Take the room**" I heard in a new voice loudly interrupting my internal dialogue. Not even my annoying mind sounded that way. I was looking right at the coyote, it wasn't him, I surveyed the street and no one was there.

"**Go with him,**" the voice said. Shit. The voice was inside my head. I shuddered as my mind finally ripped apart. Well that's it, I thought to myself. Now I'm crazy. That's it right there. Before, not crazy. Now, crazy.

"Ok, let's go," I said automatically, before I could even think about it and against my better judgment. A wry smile spread out across the coyote's face, a seeping wound.

"I'm parked right over here," he pointed towards the parking lot with his slim, bony finger.

"This is your car?!" We walked up to a cherry red, pristine condition, DeLorean.

"Yes, is there anything wrong?"

"No, I just have never seen this kind of car before in my life, I . . . I wasn't expecting it. It's, it's beautiful actually."

"Yea she's a real peach ain't she?" he said, obviously quite pleased that I was impressed by his car. So stupid, but it was true. He opened the doors that raised like bird wings into the sky. I couldn't believe this was happening. I couldn't believe the drum beat progression of life from one moment to the next. So vastly different, so unpredictable, the chaos while we are in the moments that unfold. I sat down and the seats hugged me as a comforting friend. He got in and pushed a bunch of buttons, like we were in an airplane about to go down a runway. I half expected the whole thing to lift off the ground and he would rip up his face showing me he was an alien sent here to kidnap me to colonize Mars.

"Oh shit I forgot my bike!" I said, slapping my forehead, feeling even more stupid, if that was even possible.

"*Classy,*" whispered my mind.

"Don't worry," he said in a reassuring slither, "I'll swing by and grab it tomorrow."

"Oh, that's awfully nice of you, you don't have to do that, I can take the bus back," I said, gaining discomfort being placed in a position to require anything at all from him, while simultaneously needing a lot of things from him. He flicked his cigarette out the window and lit another in the car. He rolled the window back up till it was a tiny crack, a half an inch. He was my dad in winter at that moment, I slowly smelled the tobacco filled car and transformed into that little girl, as if I was a werewolf in the full moon, riding around with daddy encased in some psychotic nostalgia. Ugh disgusting, how can God, or whatever, put me here, this is so weird. Was that the voice? That told me to get in the car? Was that God? Is God trying to punish me for taking a stripper job? Why do you do this, are you laughing somewhere? Well, fuck you God, that's what happens when you can't pay rent, if you have a problem with that do whatever you want, asshole. What are you, some kind of Machiavellian dominatrix? Well I give up, you win. Whatever.

"How cute you think God is talking to you, who's next, Napoleon? John Lennon?" Snickered my mind.

"Nah that's ok darling. No sweat. I have to head that way anyway," the coyote answered.

The way he said darling made me want to puke on his face. I always hated flattery and could feel its insincerity, a toxic high fructose corn syrup.

"Going to work?" I asked, trying to make small talk, but quickly regretted getting personal.

"Work? Haha, you're a crack up, kid. Work is for suckers. I've never had a job in my life."

Right, I thought inside my head, coyote. "Oh, sorry, I just assumed you must work to afford this car."

"Listen sweetheart, fools who work would never have this car. That's the secret. You'll meet a lot of men with jobs, they don't have this car." He wasn't wrong. There was a long pause.

"Well, aren't you going to ask me how I make my money?" he said, irritated at my disinterest and eager to show himself off.

"Oh, yea sorry," I stammered, "What do you do? Are you a trust fund kid?" I clearly had not come anywhere close to mastering the art of making money without working as the events of the evening were obvious evidence of.

"Haha, you're funny that's for sure," he whispered. "No darling, I am *not* a trust fund kid." Ugh with the darling again.

"It's just because he fancies you, darling," quipped my back-seat driver.

"I'm in the export business," he answered.

"Huh?" I asked, curious despite myself.

"Yea I just kind of, you know, travel around the world and buy stuff and then sell stuff in different places. It's the easiest gig on earth."

"What kind of 'stuff' do you sell?"

"I mean anything babe, everything I find that I think someone might want. I guess you could say I am in the business of selling desire really. I know what people want, I've always had a knack for it. Mostly I make money because I can tell people's desires, when I see things I know who will want those things." Fucking coyotes. We stopped at a red light in an intersection and there were a bunch of girls waiting to cross the street. They were visibly excited about the car and were giggling and whispering to each other, pointing and chattering, a bunch of human chipmunks.

"Hey handsome, any room for some more?" One of them crooned as she crouched down, sticking her hands between her thighs to bend over, ensuring that her bosom was visible at the lowered angle of someone seated in a vehicle.

"Maybe next time, darling!" Replied the coyote.

"*Oops, I guess you aren't his only darling.*" Mind smirked at me smugly. I let out an audible sigh and the Coyote, ever vigilant, awkwardly tried to make me feel at ease.

"Happens all the time, it's the car," he said nonchalantly. I wanted to shout at him, 'you picked me up at a strip club and yet you are somehow trying to divert your interest in other girls in front of me as if I'm an idiot'. But instead I just sat there quietly drifting out the window, ignoring his attempt to lie.

"*Not even your shitty new boyfriend respects you,*" the tormentor chirped in.

"Whatever," I accidentally said out loud, and the coyote thought I said it to him. I wondered how many people thought I was talking to them when I talked to myself and it made me laugh, which again made the coyote think it was somehow "him" related.

"Well, at least you have a sense of humor," he said. I comprehended the story of The Tower of Babel and how no one could understand each other. Everyone, really, was separated from speaking the same language as each other, it was true. I was completely alone, stranded on some alien planet like "*The Little Prince.*"

He pulled the car into a parking lot that was scarcely off the main road, the building sat practically on the street. One of the first things you lose in poverty is your privacy. Although arguably, a lot of choices go out the window, when you don't have any money, you don't have the luxury of time to yourself, or peace because you are forced into crowded situations and reliant on people who you did not choose, or would usually not spend time around simply because you do not have any other options. This motel was a perfect metaphor for so many of those losses due to lack of funds.

"Well, this is it darling, I'm friends with the owner so he gives me special rates. Let me know what you think of the art in there. I hooked him up with the goods in exchange for moments such as this, so do me a solid and give me some feedback."

"Uh, of course, no problem. Will do," I said, sincerely shocked that he cared about his work, while simultaneously curious how many girls he brought to this hotel and that he probably had the key to the room he was about to "place me in."

"Thanks a million, hey give me a second I'll be right back in two shakes of a lamb's tail."

He left the car as the door rose into the sky dramatically, epically. I must be in a science fiction novel, I thought. The motel wasn't much to look at, the sign on the front advertised "Color TVs in every room." Most places would claim Wi-Fi or pools as selling points, but wow. Color TV. I definitely slipped into some kind of a sci-fi novel, that was the only explanation really. I visibly jumped as my door opened and the coyote reached his hand up to help me out. I pretended to be un-buckling my seatbelt with both my hands to avoid touching him and he smoothly stuck his hand in his pocket. He shut the door and quick as a whip turned to place his hand in mine regardless, as he palmed me the key to the room. Both his hands wrapped around mine in an exaggerated gesture that cemented the physical contact.

"Here ya go kid, enjoy your night, I'll come by to get you in the morning and maybe to pay me back you can let me take you out for some coffee."

"Strange, I thought he said no strings attached. What else will he add to the puppet show?" Muttered my mind pointedly.

"Sounds like a plan!" I said with as much enthusiasm as I could muster, practically yanking the key from his grip as I whirled clumsily towards the door to my "room."

"My name is Willy, by the way. "He shouted after me. Shit, I thought, I'm so rude and he was trying to help me.

"Nice to meet you Willy, my name is Angela."

"Because you fell from heaven I suppose?" he shot back in the dumbest pick up stereotype I had ever heard.

"Haha, maybe" I said nervously, turning again to just get the hell away from him.

"Good night darling," he said as he disappeared into his ridiculous car, driving Lord knows where into the night.

The Arrival

I slammed the door behind me and my ears listened on high alert to make sure his car really did drive away, praying he would just leave me alone. I stood with my back pressed up against the door barely breathing, listening, waiting, hoping he would just go away. After a few minutes when I didn't notice anything, my belly let out an exhale and I folded onto the floor, grateful for the space. I could hear every car as it drove by outside, the walls were paper thin, I might as well have been on the actual street. I took in my surroundings and couldn't help but perceive the very noticeable art that decorated the room. There were huge paintings of loudly colored elephants covering the walls. Obviously from Thailand. They had a style that was unmistakable, the colors were so bizarre, they didn't belong together. Then I noticed they were the same colors as daynight. Bright orange elephants were dancing on a dark blue background.

"What are the odds of that?" I said to myself out loud. It was perhaps the ugliest art I had ever seen. I laughed despite myself, wow Willy, you sure do know what people "desire." Omg Willy. I was laughing out loud now, Will E. Coyote!!!! A perfect name, for you, *darling*. I collapsed on the bed like a building being demolished, my air escaping me, dynamited dust. The sheets were stale as crackers and the blankets scraped against my skin, coarse sandpaper. My hand fell on the side table with a thud.

"Ow!" I screamed as I jerked my hand away, the drawer rolled open from the force of it, exposing a book hidden within the unassuming piece of furniture. It was a copy of the bible. The fucking bible. It was so invading at this moment to have even the word bible enter into my consciousness much less an actual copy of a bible. There might as well have been a flashing billboard for Coca Cola above my bed. I hated the bible, always had.

"Oh, for fuck's sake!" I said out loud, even though there was no one in the room. Could this be more stupid? Is this why so many people committed suicide alone in hotel rooms with the bible on their beds? Was it out of sheer boredom of the predictability and depressing perceptibility of the lack of support from anything substantial? Did they wish to die from the burden of irony upon their dignity? Perhaps they passed out of spite for needing so much and getting only this. I pulled the book from its place and threw it on the bed. Fuck this, I thought to myself, is this some kind of prison guard, this book they place in our most private moments? Invading our intimate spaces? Shoving a bit of guilt and shame in, wherever they could. I mean what if someone was here with a prostitute? Is that why they put it in hotel rooms? One Last guilt trip right before your "sin"? What if you just wanted some time to yourself? Was this reality so purposely constructed as to prevent every last unique thought of your own and shove anything into that deep black pit of a hole?

"Open it," the voice said, luculent and not my own. It drowned out my insufferable inner dialogue with a pressure that made me jump up and stand at attention. I canvased the room, peeked behind the curtains, went into the bathroom, and I glimpsed under the bed. I couldn't see anyone.

"Open it." Again. It echoed through my bones. My mind was quiet.

Nothing to say now? I teased my mind. So chatty every other time with some sardonic comment but whatever this command was had brought you to silence. A rare experience. I clutched the book with the kind of despair that can lead to you grabbing a random bible in a hotel room in the first place. I could feel the anger well up from a depth within me that is hard to fathom. This must be where Cthulhu comes from, I thought to myself. This place. I had more alliance with Cthulhu than Jesus, that's for sure. Now I was pissed. I squeezed the tome as hard as I could, digging my fingernails into the faux leather cover until it came off revealing the white underneath.

"FAKE!" I yelled at it as loud and as long as I could until I ran out of breath. I sputtered, impotently sobbing onto the thing. They should leave *money* in the drawer, not a useless bible! What if they gave me the money they used to print this piece of shit bible! Then I would have something that would really help me! I screamed to myself. What people really needed in this God forsaken world was money so that they didn't need to spend nights in hotel rooms! I threw it down on the floor where it promptly struck my foot causing my body to collapse in pain, a curled up caterpillar on the shitty shag carpet next to the asshole book that may as well have been the Necronomicon as far as I cared. I sat up and hovered over the object, I saw my tears fall onto it, making little puddles on the pages, smearing the ink into itself. The room around me was quiet and I couldn't even hear any cars on the street outside. As I was staring at the pattern, my pity party was dribbling across the pages that had randomly opened, the words came into focus. They morphed into crisp blades out of the blurry mess.

"I am the Alpha and the Omega, the first and the last, the beginning and the end." I don't even know what that means, I sighed to myself.

"I am the beginning and the end." I gasped. The voice was responding to me in a conversation. Ok, I'll bite. Maybe this is some choose your own adventure novel and I might just be that bored with reality. Guided by my intuition, I opened the book to the first page, where it read; "In the Beginning." Oh brother, does it say "The End" at the close of the book I laughed to myself, turning to the last page.

That isn't much of a mystery to solve. Not quite. The final words were not what I was expecting.

"He which testifieth these things saith, Surely I come quickly. Amen." Was what was written there.

"I am Approaching," the voice responded. The voice boomed through my brain. Doesn't seem like an ending to me, I sneered. The book was stopping on a cliffhanger, preparing everyone for a sequel. Fucking bible, what was this shit anyways? Classic manipulation technique, keep 'em on their toes. This ending sounded more, "It ain't over yet" I laughed to myself. If this is an "ending" then I don't think the word end means what people think it means. I mean who ends a story with a non-ending. Anyway, every story has a beginning, a middle and an end.

Oh wait, there was another part. The middle. The voice had left out a vital portion. When I thought of the beginning and the end, I couldn't help but also think of; the middle. That's interesting I thought. Why not say the middle? Why name an ending that isn't an ending and leave out the middle? I spent a while pondering this, I mean a while because I am not good at math. I tried to figure out, numerically, where was the middle of this fucking story? I looked at the page numbers and tried to remember how to do basic subtraction. What is in between this clear and purposeful beginning that only has a non-committal ending. Jesus doesn't have an end, I thought to myself, there isn't even a death that is satisfactory here, the end is a dangling participle. What is the middle I wondered, despite my own disproving of the entire book and all it stood for. I am sitting here, in this hotel room trying to figure out the bible. Oh reality, you silly thing. As a child, how could I foresee that I would somehow have left my stripper job to be in a hotel room surrounded by shitty Elephants trying to figure out the bible. I must admit, I never saw *that* Disney movie.

I tried my luck, holding the book closed, and eyeballed the center. I pressed my finger hard against the pages, trying to just feel where the center was. I ran my thumb across the paper and a sharp stab caused me to pull my finger away as blood shed upon the corners of the document. A papercut, great, even this was painful. I dropped the book dramatically and it split in two, right down the middle where it landed. Just like Moses and the red sea I laughed.

It read;

"Psalm 118: Let Israel say: His love endures forever."

The middle was only another version of the refusal of an ending. So basically, the middle is predicting that there isn't an ending and then the ending is just the middle again. So, it is more the beginning, middle and beginning again. It has not actually reached the end. Hmm, a circle. It was a circle. It has not reached the end . . . I mulled that over in my mind for a while. I was daydreaming staring off into space, thinking about what that meant. That this story did not have an end. Looking at the book, I had a crazy thought. What if you take the book and touch the beginning and end together? To make a circle? What if it is all one big middle? Maybe it goes in a circle instead of a line.

I was getting excited, like when you see you are nearing the end of a jigsaw puzzle. What if you make the middle by folding the pages? Origami? I took the front of the book in my left hand and the back of the book in my right hand and tried to bend the pages towards each other. I wanted to see if it made something by joining them together. This is a Mad Magazine fold-in I thought to myself. As a child I couldn't wait to get the new ones because I wanted to solve the riddle of the fold-in on the back page. I always turned to the end first. Yes, a riddle. A secret, hidden riddle. As I tried to get the crumply paper to meet each other, with the blood from my thumb smearing all over everything, in the perfect center I stopped, staring at the pages. I could see quite clearly that when I folded the pages in to meet each other, they did make something. They formed a perfect heart shape. It was making a heart, not a circle as I had thought. I started to cry. The answer to the riddle: I am the beginning and the end, was a heart.

The heart was the answer to the riddle. Love endureth forever.

Could it be *this* stupid? Is this what people meant about Jesus ? Was it this cheesy? I was emotional none-the-less, I had literally unraveled a universal mystery all by myself, there, sitting on the floor. Sobbing now, as a child weeping for a puppy, my tears rained on the pages, mingling with and diluting the blood, as my hands quivered, holding them in place. I couldn't tell if the pages were shaking my hands or my hands were shaking the pages, and then all the air left me and I could not take a breath. A sucker punch to the gut. The atmosphere accumulated density, did I fall asleep and forget? Am I dreaming? I couldn't move. I closed my eyes and opened them again but the book was still convulsing in front of me, I recoiled my hands back, violently releasing the heart shaped pages but they stayed right where they were.

"Impossible," I whispered, my eyes grew three sizes, pressing my eyelids back into my head. I thought I imagined it at first, a slight change in the position of the book, but now it moved in a more purposeful fashion. It was trying to turn around, in a circle. I could not avert my gaze though quickly forming fear sweat was pouring into my eyes. I caught in my periphery that some other objects in the room were moving too. The curtains were starting to drift in towards the growing cyclone and chairs were inching across the floor, despite the formidable carpet.

My hair was blowing in my face, sticking to my damp cheeks as a wind spiraled in the center of the room, though there were no open windows. The gale was coming from inside the book. I sat contorted in disbelief as the tornado commenced to form real circles and spirals launching into a full-blown twister in the shitty hotel room. Blueish white sparks of electricity spilled over my head from the ceiling until a bolt of lightning struck the Color TV on the table in the corner.

"Oh my God!" I yelled and covered my head. *BOOM*, the sound of thunder split the room. This is totally out of hand, I tried to approach the book to stop it, but a knife of lightning cut through me, it knocked me flat and splayed me out on the floor. All I could do was stare at the gathering cloud that was stretching across the expanse of the room, opening a hole into outer space. A dense shadow proceeded to take over the ceiling with a sparkly darkness behind it. I could only lay there, experiencing it. Then, quiet as a mouse, almost in slow motion, a man fell from the sky onto the floor next to me. Ploop.

It was over. As quickly as it had begun, it had ended. Everything was motionless now, as if time had stopped. I was laying staring into the face of the naked man who was wrapped in a glow like a baby in a blanket on the shit brown carpet of the Motel. His eyelids fluttered, as his pupils rolled around a few times before catching my face, instantly he was sitting straight up, sinewy, a panther.

"You did it!" he shouted in disbelief. The voice . . . it was him. The same voice that had guided me to take the room, to get in the car. Emanating from it I sensed a primordial presence which had lived long before being placed here, in front of me now.

"You solved it. I'm free! Do you have any idea how long I have been waiting for someone to figure that out?" He laughed and shook some kind of ectoplasmic goo from his hair. He was totally naked. He was beautiful.

"What do you mean figure it out? Figure what out?" I quizzed as if I knew anything at all anymore, or could possibly understand anything he answered me with.

"You released me. You got me out."

"You were *in* the book?

"In a way, yes."

"What just happened? What is going on?" I hyperventilated, becoming too aware that I was speaking with someone, something that had just materialized out of nowhere.

"I guess there is no one left who even knew we were in there. This room seems new. I am unfamiliar with these smells," he said, trailing off as his eyes wandered around the room, squinting a bit in distaste as they saw the tacky elephant paintings.

"We? There are more of you in there?" I didn't even know where to start. The feeling of something far beyond my reach was gathering into the mother of all panic attacks in my chest.

"Quite a few combinations, yes."

"Combinations?"

"The letters, the letters on the pages of the book. When you fold them together, we unfold. I guess no one folds the pages anymore. Who would have thought it would be so easy to conceal simply because no one would ever even think to do it after a while? Amazing how forgetful everyone is over time. Everything changes over time, yes."

"Are you trying to tell me that if you do origami to the pages of the bible that more of you will pop out?"

"Yes, when the letters touch," he said, realizing how very little I seemed to know. He looked at me more deeply as though I were a child that he was teaching in kindergarten.

"Who are you? What is happening? Am I dead?" I said a little too loudly, trying to catch my breath.

"I am Asher," he said as he looked at me with eyes that felt like eons. I couldn't keep up with what was happening, my mind was rebelling, a toddler throwing a tantrum. Was I making this up in my head? I thought in my mind. How is he speaking English, what is happening? Is he real?

"I am real" was the answer. I looked around the room to see if it was still there since he had captured all of my attention. There was a mirror on the wall over the dresser and I could catch part of his reflection in it. It didn't look the same as he appeared when I stared directly at him. It was off, his image in the mirror was moving like water, he was a different shape, it looked like he had . . . ears on top of his head. A creep ran up my spine. I was trying to look closer but he quickly changed the subject.

"I am here with you" Was the reply. His lips did not move, he was speaking directly into my head. I could hear his voice. I forgot how to speak. I could only take in information, my head was reeling in circles faster than the tornado that landed him here. Him? I think he was a him, he seemed to be a man, but also didn't quite feel like a man. It was more a genderless feeling, as if he had no lower nature. Pretty much the exact opposite of the coyote, who was all lower nature. He had no nature at all. I wouldn't even call him supernatural. He was more . . . .robotic if I am being honest.

"I am not a robot," he said with no emotion at all and honestly as a robot would.

I lost my pace as I caught up with everything that just happened. I was dredging through sludge and my mind and body were left behind about thirty minutes ago and were just now running up the steps to join us in all this.

"It's the delay. Don't worry, you seem to process at a faster rate than most. I'll give you a moment. I am surprised you could hear me and even more surprised that you listened to me. No one ever listens to me. They usually can't even hear me. It is rare to find those who listen and follow."

"What do you mean delay?" I shot out finally, my curiosity overriding my awestruck confusion.

"You, you humans are in the past. You are never quite 'in the time.' Some are worse than others. Some of you have taken great efforts and practices to remedy it, but as a species you remain terribly late in general, it's quite irritating from my perspective. Imagine talking to someone overseas on a bad computer and there is a two minute lag, you wouldn't even be able to handle it." He was speaking so frankly and matter of factly, as though we were friends, like he knew me, it made me feel weird inside. He was very familiar with me, but he was an alien. How did he know about computers and lags?

"I saw it in yourself."

"Do we know each other?" I asked childishly. Do I know him? What the hell is wrong with me, he just fell out of a ceiling tornado.

"Ugh you are such an idiot," said my mind assailant, piping up for the first time in quite a while. Asher turned quickly to me and stared just over my shoulder. My spine wildly twisted and I fell to the ground in a seizure.

"Listen, we need to be leaving soon, I know there are a lot of questions you will have for me. Humans spend so much time asking questions instead of just living or observing, it's rather maddening. It might be what sets you behind in time, come to think of it. Before we go, we are going to have to do something about him though," he mumbled under his breath averting his eyes, as he knelt down beside me on the ratchet carpet.

"What? Him who? Who are you talking about?" I asked completely clueless, while realizing he had just made fun of me for asking questions. Annoyed with my human frailty, I frantically searched the room with my eyes. Did I miss someone else falling from the ceiling tornado? I would have a freaking heart attack if there were two of them. Were we going to have a spaceman fight, or what?

"Him." He said, as he pointed directly into the center of my forehead. His finger made contact like an arrow and ran me straight through. A thing squirmed deep within my pink brain mass and I promptly threw up all over the shag. It turns out my body just couldn't take the sensation of some kind of brain worm wriggling around inside it. As much as we imagine we will be stoic when such things happen, our inner hero complex fantasies always fall so far from the realities of the naked truth, I thought to myself, scrying helplessly into my stomach contents.

"Unnnngggghh, wha . . . what's happening?" I choked out as I gagged from the pain. The weird feeling was too much. Terrified at the autonomous capacity of my body, which was moving as it saw fit rather than listening to me at all, I lurched into a fetal position and convulsed regardless of my opinions about the matter. Deathly stillness settled like snow in the room, like a curtain falling after a play. I wasn't moving, not even breathing, but I could see and hear everything.

I was trapped. There was a moist mist emitting from my mouth that was condensing into fog as it hit the air. The temperature had dropped and I thought I saw snowflakes forming out of the oxygen in the air around me. All I could do was stare as the smoke thickened and gathered into a whirlpool. The center of the now pitch-black plume was crackling and sparking with miniature lightning bolts shooting out of it. A form was taking shape and wings sprouted out of the cyclone. I gazed in awe at the clearly sentient being that was emerging and co-agulating out of my body. It hovered like a bird over my face. With a dramatic and audible flap of its expanse I could make it out, it was a manta ray with glowing red eyes. The graceful Marine apparition turned its face towards me and looked right into my eyes. It had a voice that spoke directly into me without using sound or words.

"Guess we've both been evicted now, way to go. Well, it's been nice tagging along. I'll keep my eyes on you and maybe we'll meet again some-day." The voice was unmistakable, my mind asshole, I would know it anywhere. I broke free of the motionless moment I had been imprisoned in with an audible gasp. The thought, in my now apparently clear mind, that part of my inner voice had not been mine was causing my entire being to inflame in insult. The thing wisped towards the door like smoke and turned into a translucent glimmering shimmer, and disappeared into the wall as if it wasn't even there. My stomach heaved and coughed spasmodically. I think I had a little chunk of puke in my nose. I tried to get myself together. I couldn't really lift my head for a minute so I took a few deep long breaths, intimately engaging the smells of the forlorn flooring.

"What was that? Who was that? some kind of monster? Was that part of me, am I some kind of monster?" I spat out the flurry of un-wanted questions in a heave of effort, sputtering bubbles from my lips, writing in a sweaty pile on the absorbent carpet.

"It was a parasite," he stated matter of factly, as you would answer a question on a test.

"What?" I saw him roll his eyes, obviously irritated at my recalcitrant, incessant questions.

"It was a parasite. Think of it like a vampire. Only a vampire that lives inside you and sucks your blood slowly and forever. It is a creature, one that lives within you but isn't really you."

"What? How long has it been there? A while? Do other people have them?" All I could think about was how gross it was that I had a parasite and I was trying to talk as much as I could so that I wouldn't throw up again.

"Yes, yes they do."

"What?"

"It turns out it's quite a problem for human beings."

"Will it come back?" I shivered at the thought of that thing crawling back into me and my stomach made sure to let me know how little it enjoyed that train of thought.

"Not while I'm here."

"How long are you going to be here? I nervously asked the naked ceiling tornado man.

"I don't know, we will have to wait and see."

"I, I thought it was part of me. I mean, it was a different voice in my head, but I just always thought that it was my inner critic or something."

"Yes, they do that, they love to hide, they influence people to talk about things like inner critics, rather interesting if you think about it. They are quite clever, I guess that is why humans wanted them around, they thought it would make them smarter, give them some kind of advantage, an edge. Oh, humanity, so much amusement can be found in your actions seeking to improve upon what you perceive to be flawed while you make things worse in the process. It is quite a tragedy when you can see it."

"How could I not see it, I mean how do we not see them?" I felt ashamed that he could see it and I couldn't, as though I were flawed, much like he had just mentioned.

"I'm not sure, it's really quite obvious to me."

"What?"

"I can see and hear them very clearly."

"How come no one ever talks about those things? Why do you get to see them and I can't?"

"They do, they are mostly called demons."

"What?"

"Demons, they are demons."

"Well what are you called? Wait, what are you? What does the name Asher mean?" My mind was, at this point, completely immersed in its confusion and it was frantically grabbing at Asher who was the only way out of this whirlpool of cluelessness.

"It's hard to explain because it means many things at the same time. Mostly, it means a leap of faith, but it also means a prisoner." He shrugged his shoulders in the first slightly emotional nuance I had noticed from him.

"Where do you leap to?" I asked.

"Into the fire. Very well then, that's taken care of, time to go. I know you have more questions, but this is very boring for me, I'm sure you understand. Just try and relax and go with the flow, if that is helpful. Try and quiet your mind now."

"Yes, time to go," I replied, even though I had no idea where we were going, who he was, what he was talking about and he still didn't answer. What did he mean, prisoner? I might have just inadvertently freed some ex-con of the universe who had committed a heinous crime.

"Mind your mind, I can hear everything you say. You think that just because you are unable to perceive the mind of another that it must be so for all. Every creature can hear everything you constantly whistle out of there. I know you can't help it, but I'm going to have to ask you to remember to keep yourself silent as much as you can. Just try and be quiet. There are plenty of other holes in your head you can use other than your mouth. All you do is sit around trying to figure everything out, while filling the space for an answer to enter with noise of your own making. This is not a big math problem or assignment for you, the truth and answers you seek are spread before you in full sight."

"Uh, so you can hear all my thoughts?" I asked, still trying to catch up, noticing it might be impossible for me to follow his instructions.

"Yes, you can hear all of mine too if you listen, you can hear the trees and the wind if you listen. You are far too accustomed to listening to yourself and those parasites that perch on your shoulders. You at least heard me, and listened to what I said. I know you can do this, I know you can listen, that is why this is happening to you, because you listened." He saw through me and I felt naked, without skin, I was an amoeba being stared at in a petri dish.

"I understand it isn't your fault, I am not blaming you, there is no choice of yours that led here. The parasites were a choice your ancestors made a long, long time ago. They've been there so long I'm not sure they can be extracted from people unless I am around. Most humans would die of shock during the removal process."

"You mean I could have died?"

"No not you, I was there."

"Oh . . ."

"Shamans, priestesses or exorcisms work occasionally, but the people usually die, or find they are unable to assimilate with others afterwards."

"Why would my ancestors choose to have these things with them?"

"They serve certain purposes."

"Like what?"

"They have a mind of their own so it gives you two minds, the only problem is they mostly only want to think for themselves. They take the human over so they drive the actions, rather than sharing the choices with the other. They are very selfish . . . which is why they are a parasite. They cannot cohabitate. They make humans selfish."

"Why?"

**"I'm afraid that now I must insist upon departure, I under-
stand your constant questions are inherent to your predicament,
however, we need to go,"** he said, opening the door and heading into
the night.

A Novel Approach

Stepping out of the door was an assault. The light was too bright. Everything was wrong and loud. Even though it was the middle of the night, the Sun was out. Daynight, I thought, snickering to myself, though it wasn't dusk. Where was the light coming from? It seemed to be all around, but I couldn't find the source, there was no Sun out, there seemed to be light emitting from everything in a chorus or symphony. I could hear every sound in infinite detail. For a moment I thought I could see the sound, rippling through the atmosphere. Far away, or close, I wasn't sure, I heard an insect. Normally it would sound like a buzz, but now, it was more like a vibration, a drum beat pounding over distance to arrive inside my ear. I thought I could tell what kind of insect it was because of how it sounded, I could see its shape from the wave of sound filling me. It landed on a tree nearby, it was a fly, I could feel the shape of the tree, sense it from the wave made with the sound from the fly's wings hit the surface of the bark. This must be what echolocation is like, I thought. The tree felt like it noticed me feeling its shape and I could sense its awareness turn towards me, like in my direction and the fly too turned its mind upon me. Nothing was private, everything knew and sensed each other in the naked air. I could smell . . . so many things. My nose could see as well, the scents entering me carried so much information. I caught a whiff of the fly, the tree, my own body. I felt like I had eyes over every inch of my flesh. Everything was moving, alive and shaking, vibrating. Waves and ripples were hitting me from every direction. The whole world was underwater, flowing, moving and raw. Every breath became a death as I tried to hold everything still, questing for quiet in every footfall.

"**What's wrong?**" Asher's voice invaded in a shout, but he was probably just speaking at a regular volume, it was my own distress causing the amplification. My own newness to this experience.

"I didn't . . . I didn't know everything was so loud and weird," I purposefully whispered, afraid to use the full volume of my own voice. It must have sounded louder inside of me than it did outside of me. I had no perception of self vs other anymore and was so diluted with my own sense organs everything had been inverted.

"**Interesting, it seems the parasite made you very muddy. What you are feeling is the clarity of your perceptions after I removed the demon. You are experiencing life as it actually is, without the filter of the parasite.**"

"What? You mean this is how it's going to be now?" I freaked. I wanted to quit. How could I live like this now? It was too much I wanted out, where was the escape hatch.

"**You will adjust to it. As all things, we adapt to circumstances. Although it will be quite a bit more intense in every way now. Coming into true reality is the best, however difficult. I don't recommend replacing the parasite.**"

"No wonder people seek out demons! If it means this shit is turned down, I get why someone would make the choice, this is insane! Anything to make it stop!" I complained.

"**Yes, insane . . .**" He trailed off as his eyes fixed upon the distance, he was clearly done coddling me.

A fly flew by and I looked into its eye, I saw a hundred other eyes inside the large one, as if they went on forever in an infinite iteration.

Something was coming out of it that wasn't noise, it was . . . something else, something strange. Felt like a color, I could sense it was in response to me. Ugh! It was thinking! I could feel the thoughts of the fly as it passed me, it was invading my space like someone spilling water over me. Its thoughts were so loud I couldn't ignore them to focus on something else, a breeze lilted from its wings, I understood its destination while simultaneously the cosmic rays from the moon were hitting my skin. I was losing my mind. I had become hyper aware of everything. My skull was going to explode from overstimulation.

"Take some deep breaths, that might help you," he said, conscientiously, but with a condescending tone, lowering his voice trying to comfort my newly found sensitivity. I could feel everything, and it was terrible. I crouched down, hugging my knees and tried to count as I inhaled and exhaled repeatedly, slowing my pace at each breath. I couldn't look at the pavement too long or I would get caught up in it, I could see specs of different kinds of stones, marbled together in intricate detail, it was beautiful, like a painting. I had to close my eyes and try to stay with my breath, stay where I was. I looked around, still counting my breath. Asher was standing there, I could feel him getting impatient. It was very apparent he was very naked, and we very much had no way to get anywhere. He was completely clueless of this fact. I mean he was just heading off, buck ass naked into the world and I was like, wait though. Maybe pants. I tried to drop back down into normal brain which said, yes, he will need some pants.

"Ahem," I spoke at last, clearing my throat, I could feel my esophagus rumbling as the words emerged, I had certainly never felt that before, I think the only time I ever have had any inclusion of the inside of my body is when it was in pain. How interesting I could only feel when there was pain I mused. He turned without saying anything and just peered into my face. And when I say into my face, I mean into my face, I got a sickening sensation that he was staring through me as though I were transparent and he was considering the space behind me. He looked down at his body indicating he already heard what I was about to say. He directed his mind to my body, at my clothing. His thoughts resembled a finger pointing, I could feel it take shape as his mind formed his intention.

"Do you have more of those?" he asked, motioning towards my clothes.

"I mean, I have *my* clothes," I answered him, "But they are at my storage unit. Fuck, how are we even going to get you there? You have to understand, I mean I don't know where exactly you come from, but you can't walk around naked here. It's a problem, no one walks around naked here, it will draw . . . negative attention," I explained.

"Hmm yes, I understand. I have been naked for so long, I have removed it from my concern."

"Ok, ok hang on let me figure this out. Shit I don't even have any money either. I mean I can somehow get to the storage place, maybe there is a bus, but I don't think you are going to fit into my clothes and they are clothes for women."

"Why is that important?"

"It's just that you are going to stand out, well, stand out even more than you obviously would, there is ignorance and hate projected towards men who choose to dress in women's clothing, I have no idea why I mean the fact that people feel they can project upon others is really something in this day and age, but regardless, you can totally wear my clothes if you want, we just won't go unnoticed is all," I reasoned.

"Very well, we must wait for your friend now," he said, as though I would know what the hell he was talking about.

"What? What friend, what are you talking about?"

"The one who brought you here."

"What, why? He's not my friend either!"

"Sigh, for the clothes, he will come and you will go with him. I will hide in the room." I felt like Asher had somehow fast forwarded through the rest of the night and could see what was going to happen.

"What? How do you . . . How do you know that?"

"I can see everything, nothing is hidden. I see all of time and space, it is all transparent, see through, I guess you would call it. I can see everything that is going to happen, don't you get it? Imagine we are in a car. I am driving the car, and I have mirrors everywhere, ahead of me I see the future, behind me I see the past, next to me I see the now, only I can see them all at once, an eye for every angle." I just stood there quietly with my jaw slack.

"And me? What can I see?"

"You are in the trunk of the car. All is dark around you."

"Right." He went back into the room, while I leaned up against the wall and slid down to my knees to wait.

THE EXCHANGE

I needed the coyote. I just had to accept it. This is what it had come down to. Understanding and realizing that I had to get help from a coyote, even with a super special naked spaceman entering the picture. Damnit, I hate this. Fucky fuckity fuck. I waited outside alone while Asher stayed in the room. My thoughts were all over the place trying to answer all the questions that kept spawning more questions in an infernal cycle that I feared could continue until the end of time. I tried to keep reminding myself what Asher had said about being silent but I was coated in my mind like a thick rubber garment that was suffocating the life out of me. I wasn't sure what was worse, my thoughts or the inundation with perceptual vibrations threatening to implode me from their force. Kept returning to counting my breath as that seemed to put things down to a low boil. I exaggerated the numbers as I inhaled, putting force on them while I counted, trying to listen to the rasp of my lungs as they pulled in the air. Something shifted and I felt things change, as though a gear had turned to fall into a slot. I perked up my ears and heard the rumble of a vehicle approaching.

The coyote turned the corner and pulled up, into the parking spot. I heard his car coming from blocks away in the silence of the morning and with my newly attuned ears. He saw me, smiled, with the Sun rising behind him as he got out of the DeLorean, the door ascended into the air with a hydraulic hiss, it was like a postcard from the 80's, picture perfect. The sky was the reverse of my favorite time, I had never seen it because I'm usually asleep at the butt crack of dawn. It was the reverse of daynight. It was nightday. All I could think about now was the damn elephant paintings, as the memory of them swept mockingly into my thoughts. How strange is this device of mind, that I am its servant rather than it mine, I pondered as the coyote made his approach.

That's when I saw it. His parasite. I visibly jumped, in primal terror, like a hand pulling away from a hot stove. It was so apparent, so plain for me to see now, it was hard to believe that the fucking thing had just been sitting there the whole time I had been talking to him and that I was completely clueless. I had one too while we were having our conversations, my mind twisted and lurched at the recall. Hold it together, I told myself. He was getting closer, I felt his steps hit the pavement like bass drums turned up so loud they made a fuzz. The panic hit me, and I broke out into a sweat as he met my eyes and I tried, so, so hard, to look at him and not the gargoyle sitting perfectly upon his shoulder. But I couldn't help it, I fucked up. I looked at it. I stared right into its red, beady little eyes. It saw me see it. It knew that I knew.

The feeling of it seeing me see it filled us both with fear. A wash of horror struck through the fucking thing, as it squirmed and squished its way around to his back trying to hide behind his head. I watched it change its shape to conform to the shape of his silhouette, so that no part of it was sticking out and the color of it darkened to blackness, an octopus trying to camouflage itself as a shadow, hiding behind him, hoping I might mistake it for some trick of the light or a patch of random darkness. So clever, I thought to myself, aren't you slick. Meanwhile, the coyote had turned into a statue while his guest tried to burrow into his neck. The coyote felt it move, I could see that he experienced it. His eyes had a glaze to them, traveling somewhere very far away despite whatever might be directly in front of his face. He tilted his head to the side like a dog trying to listen to something high pitched.

"That's weird," he announced. "Did you feel that?" he asked me, still standing in the exact same spot, his foot raised half off the ground in mid step.

"Feel what?" I asked him back, I was a really bad actress. He could tell I was faking.

"Huh, never mind I guess." He took the few steps left to close the distance between us. He looked into my eyes for the first time and froze again, his foot halfway off the ground.

"You're different" The coyote whispered, squinting his eyes. He was searching all over me, as if his inspection would uncover some hidden clue. His eyes turned into magnifying glasses that could burn a hole in an ant.

"What happened to you? What is this, what is going on? Why do I feel so strange?" he persisted, raising his voice slightly in alarm.

"What do you mean?" I had always been a bad liar. The coyote was too savvy though. Gotta give them that, intuitive as the day is long those fucking coyotes, they never skip a beat. They can smell shit on the wind from a hundred miles away. They had their own kind of power and this coyote was no different even if he did have a demon on his shoulder diming his shine. He didn't say anything and just kept looking at me trying to solve the puzzle with his x-ray specs, like someone staring at a Rubik's cube to reveal the pattern. I had to try my very hardest not to focus on his parasite, although all I really wanted to do was rudely stare at his demon, to examine it in detail while I had the chance. Ugh I had no idea how difficult this integration was going to be. I was the only one in on a secret that I couldn't tell for fear of complete and total isolation as well as being placed within some kind of mental health facility. It hit me that I may never be able to talk to people again, I could feel discomfort coating my throat like a flu. As I struggled trying to figure out what to do and how to handle this in my mind, he spoke and said;

"Why don't you just tell me what's going on. I can feel this is batshit crazy off and I don't need any crazy, I know what I feel." His words spilled out of his stern face. I could feel him getting angry now. If there is one thing coyotes hate, it's when they can't figure out what's going on. A gentleman is true to his nature, after all.

"I know you feel it, and I'm so sorry but I can't tell you what it is. The reason I can't tell you is because it's too insane, but here is what I will say; You are right, you do feel something, something very big, you are not crazy, it's the thing that has happened that is crazy. I am not going to tell you what it is to keep *you* from going crazy ok? I'm going to keep it to myself and the reason I am going to keep it to myself is because I am being courteous to you. I am also going to say I wish you *did* know what I know and I think that everyone needs to know what I know and I think it's possibly the most important thing that everyone needs to know and I don't know anybody who knows this!" I abruptly blurted out. Yep, I definitely am going to be put in a psych ward.

"Slow down kid, you sound like you just saw Jesus." His response made me burst out howling.

"Oh man," I said to him, "you have no idea how hilarious what you just said is. Does the Alpha and Omega count?" Psychic coyote powers on full display, he could feel something of what I meant but he just didn't know what it was. "I'm going to get back to you on that ok? I'm just going to have to get back to you on that. Just trust me, for now you aren't in any danger and you are right, your feeling is right ok?"

"Not in danger for *now*?" His face dilated, angrier by the second. He took a deep breath in while I watched a tentacle from his parasite move into his hair. He scratched his head on the spot, clueless to the cause. My hands clenched into fists as I tried to hide my reaction.

"Ok kid. Ok, I'll wait," he said, dropping his eyes, giving up.

"Thanks, you won't regret it. So, I need a favor," I said, cringing my face into the cutest smile I could muster like a naughty child. Now he flushed and was fully pissed. I could see that I had triggered him.

"Hmm!" he shouted, "you mean more than the favors I have already given you, right? Darling, I'm not a fool, I know a vampire when I see one." My laughter popped like popcorn as I glimpsed at the mind vampire attached to his neck. He was confused and silent. He stared at his feet, I could see his mind trying to calculate the possible explanations of the data he was receiving that was scrambling his circuitry.

"Something is up, I don't know what is so hilarious, I admit that was a rude thing to say, but I know this is weird and now you are asking me for things. Everyone has their limits."

"Don't you even want to know what I need?" I offered, innocently.

"What is it, Angela?" he said, defeated. He never called me by my name, he always called me sweetheart, or darling, not my name. It made an impact on me as a direct reference rather than impersonal.

"I need to get a change of clothes from my storage unit, and I need a ride. That's all, I just need a ride."

"Oh. That's it?" he said, raising his left eyebrow into the shape of a question mark. He was clearly suspicious and not sure if I was going to stab him or something when we got into his car. Funny, that's how I had felt the first time I took a ride from him.

"Yes, that's all I swear," I said, kind of lying since I had no clue what else was going to happen or what I would need.

"I'm sorry, I got thrown off by how weird you feel. Get in, we can go get your clothes."

"Thank you, really I owe you one." I gave him a hug without thinking about it, but jerked my whole body away because I could feel his vampire when I put my hands on his back, and his parasite moved again, spiraling him into contortion.

"What the fuck was that?!" he yelled at me, grabbing my arms with a desperate look in his eyes.

"*That* is the thing I cannot tell you about," I said very seriously and flatly. He took a few steps back, staring at me trying so hard to figure it out. I saw the problem of humans. This must be Asher's view as well. I saw that he was trying to figure it out, but he could only use what he had in his mind to do that. How is one supposed to figure something out if half the picture is missing? It's impossible! A simple reveal shows everything, but we are all so in the dark! There was no way, given all the time and intelligence in the world he would see this, because he had no idea there was a parasite feeding off him. One simple blind spot was blocking the entirety of his view of the truth.

"Don't worry, you can't know this, it isn't some failing on your part. I wish I didn't know, trust me. Maybe someday you can know too, and wish you could forget it," I said, wishing I could forget it and pretend I was normalish again. He was visibly unsettled, off his confidence. I had not seen him off. He was totally insecure, like how I usually felt and had when I first met him.

"Just, just get in the car Angela." I saw his hands shake as he reached for his keys.

We pulled back up to the hotel in a surreal Deja vu after the painfully silent journey to procure the fashion challenged outfit I was about to bestow upon the whatever the fuck it was waiting in the room. I was relieved it was over and hoped I could just turn into a pillar of salt so that I never had to talk to him again.

"I'll wait in the car while you go in and change," the coyote said, while his creepy creature slithered around ceaselessly, uncomfortable at my seeing it but unwilling to leave its host.

"Ok, one sec," I said, having no idea how we were going to evade him now. There is no way, unless Asher could somehow evaporate into nothingness and transport us somewhere, wherever the fuck he was going, shit where we were going. I could feel his parasite watching me as I exited the spacecraft-esque car and made a prompt bee-line for the room. I approached the door and was filled with dread. I broke out in a sweat. I didn't want any of this. All I wanted to do was run away. Why did that voice tell me to come here? Why is this happening to me? I was certain that the coyote was gonna start freaking out if I took too long, but I also didn't want to face Asher again, because I had no idea what he was or what he was going to do and I trembled. I did not feel safe, I was trapped. I stood there as a stranger who had never seen a door before and didn't know what to do. I had to go in. There was no other choice now, I had no decision in the matter. You would think

that might be comforting, to not have a choice, to feel free and liberat-
ed from responsibility due to the eradication of all other options, but
it wasn't. I slowly turned the knob and entered. It took me a second
to adjust, taken aback at first and shocked because the whole room
looked like it had been hit by a tornado. Oh yea, I guess it had been.
The bed was turned over, sheets tossed about, furniture overturned.
Shoot, I was going to get in trouble.

"That should be the last worry on your mind right now." I
jumped as Asher's voice boomed into the room. He was standing directly beside me, still naked and slightly shining.

**"Do not be afraid. Always the unknown causes you humans so
much fear. Knowing is not what satisfies fear. Even if I told you
everything, even if you understood the entire universe it wouldn't
help you. It is coming into a deep understanding that your fear
makes no difference to the course of events, that is what brings fear
to its end."** I just eyeballed the floor and placed the garbage bag full of
garments at his feet for him to choose from. The last thing I wanted to
do was dress him up like a doll. He chose the brightest weirdest outfit
you could possibly imagine and pulled it over his body like a toddler
putting on their sibling's clothes. The pants were girl's pants and so
did nothing to hide the visible outline of his man parts. There was
nothing left to the imagination and was pretty much the same as if he
was naked. I just didn't bother saying anything. The clothes were way
too small for him and the sleeves landed half way up his arms and the
pants were riding high giving him a camel toe.

"Now what? He is waiting for me outside," I asked nervously, trying
not to shit talk his appearance.

**"I understand your discomfort but it is unnecessary. If I ap-
proach him, his parasite will leave and we will have to bring him
with us, if he lives,"** Asher said, sociopathically.

"So what is your plan? I mean how are we going to get out of here?
He is going to be weird and want to know who you are, which I mean,

I can't really answer that myself," I said, fishing, hoping he would explain something, anything to me.

"**We are going through the window. Follow me.**" He darted for the bathroom unusually fast, like an animal, like a cat, without waiting for me to answer or have any input. I saw his form through the bathroom mirror and I swear I saw . . . a black animal for a brief moment. He opened the window and was half way out before I made it over there. He jumped onto the grass below. And motioned for me to follow him with his mind.

The Lullaby

We were running down the street in full view for all to see, a couple of weirdos, or criminals. I was an alien and everything was a counterfeit. The light was too bright. The world was like a theater set. I was seeing tracers coming off of everything as I moved, my perception was a projector showing a film too slow. My mind was going faster than my body and I could see through the cinema. Frames of movement were a sequential line of animation stills. This was a new feeling. Not even a panic attack, a full-blown dissociation. I was in the world but completely separate from it simultaneously, the whole thing was going to crack right down the middle and I would be able to see what was behind it. This was what all those people who used the phrase "beyond the veil" were talking about. There was a concealed existence behind what we were running through. We passed some people. Their parasites were visible, they jumped as we passed, recoiling. At first, I thought it was because of me, but then I realized it was because of him, Asher. What did I do, what have I done? The enormity of him was beyond my comprehension. This was dangerous, serious, like a bomb going off. Asher was a bomb.

The parasites were disturbed by him. I reckoned that if we weren't running, if he was walking or we were standing still, they would all just be forced to leave and all the people would die. At least the ones nearby. The people were all so dampened, so sad. I couldn't believe I didn't notice before. We were all just walking around in this state of being, sleepwalking and it was regular. My whole life was a trick, what else did I not know? Apparently, a lot! The vast expanse of all my ignorance sent me into a miasma. The betrayal of everything I had ever known, I had been raised in a cave and was just witnessing my first sunrise.

"Hurry up, this way," he said, speeding along, it was all I could do to keep up with him. I was getting tired. I was never very good at running. I kept trying to focus on placing one foot down, then the other, treading each and every moment through my feet. I was having flashbacks to highschool gym class and the dread of having to run in front of everybody. I always lagged behind. The first time I got my period was in middle school while running and it was among the worst experiences of my life, until now, obviously. We went off the main path into a small wooded area. He slowed down, reducing his pace to a walk, after running forever. We had to run, the consequence of his effect on the people would have been devastating.

"Where are we going? Can we stop to rest? Can you just tell me what is going on?" I asked with increasing desperation. Everything he said was right and he came from a black hole, but I just couldn't deal, I had to know what was going on. All I ever did was ask him questions and I got annoyed with myself. He stopped abruptly as we came to a small clearing. I looked over the edge of what appeared to be a pretty gnarly cliff.

"You must sleep here," he said forcefully, pointing to the precipice. there was a near thousand-foot shear wall and the drop to the sea below and my mouth uncontrollably dangled open.

"What? I can't sleep here? That's not how it works. Do you even sleep? Do you know what you are talking about? Do you know what you are asking me? Plus it's daytime now, it's too bright. There is no way I am going to fall asleep here unless you shoot me with a tranquilizer gun full of Xanax, it is *way* too stressful. I'm going to be too busy shitting my pants to be sleeping, if I roll over I could fall to my death. No, no way.”

“It is true, I do not sleep. That is why I need you to do something for me. It is not possible for me to enter into a state of sleeping. I am awakened. To be awakened means you never sleep. To be able to sleep means you are still able to go under, to go below, to die. Those who slumber are still in the underworld. I will never be able to go to the underworld again . . . unaided.”

“What do you mean unaided? Underworld? You mean Hell? Am I in Hell right now, that would explain a lot actually,” I replied, seriously considering this possibility.

“I mean I cannot get in by myself. I need someone to get me in.”

“God? Divine intervention, or what? I don’t get it. How does me sleeping have anything to do with you?”

“No, Angela, I need you. I need you to get me into the underworld.” I broke out in a cold sweat. Goosebumps danced across my skin at his words. Fear flooded me. He called me by my name, he used my name. I had a very specific feeling crawl into my belly button. I kept thinking about how the coyote called me by my name. Something important was happening, I could feel it but I didn’t know what it was. Like feeling the wind for the first time while not knowing what the wind was. I was nagged that a terrible thing would happen if I did what he said, maybe the whole world would explode. Asher was a nuclear bomb.

“You are afraid,” he said. Oh, the joys of the reality of full transparency! Haha no wonder no one wants to be enlightened, this is horrible and embarrassing. I could hide nothing.

“It is your need to hang onto your embarrassment that keeps you from entering the upper realms. Your humiliations keep you humble and bound to the earth and the underworld. If only you could make a departure from shame once and for all.” I deeply hated that he could hear every thought I had, I couldn’t even pay attention to what he was saying.

"I think that what you think is the underworld and what I think is the underworld are two very different things. That's what I think. There is no way I can just go to the underworld I am thinking about by falling asleep. And I have no clue how I am supposed to get you in there either."

"At least you didn't ask a question," he said sarcastically.

"Yes. Be cautious of stories, they deviate from truth which is observable. The underworld is accessible if you have not unified your subconscious mind. It is not Hell, although, to me it certainly is Hell to not be unified. You are in it while you are awake, because you are not really awake. You are sleeping even now, and you don't even know it. But for you, perhaps you have never wondered what it is that happens when you fall asleep."

"What are dreams then?" He was right, I hadn't ever thought about it. Sleep just happened, like peeing.

"I cannot explain everything to you Angela, somethings you have to figure things out for yourself or your own mind shall become stunted. Imagine constantly focusing on a cellular phone and then abruptly have to look up and deal with an elephant charging at you. It will not serve you to simply make me answer everything your thoughtless mind can think up. Just look around, consider and observe instead of questioning."

"Ugh, this is so hard."

"I know. Just listen. I need you to go somewhere in your dreams."

"What? That's not how it works, you don't get to choose where you go in dreams, you are taken places, it's more of a ride."

"It's a ride for you, you mean, that doesn't mean that's how it is, or how it is for me. You can choose where you go in your dream. Just be quiet and understand that there is much that you do not know, is that too much to ask?"

"*I* cant!"

"You *can*. Stop arguing with me, you are like a child saying ing they can not do something because they haven't before,

think about it. Listen, I will give you instructions, let me finish. I need you to go somewhere in your dream and perform a task, that is how you will be able to get me in the underworld, it's that simple. I need you to open a door, if that makes sense."

"Ok," I said, trying not to sound stupid. "Why do you need to go to the underworld?" I really couldn't stop the questions, I really couldn't.

"Because, that is where everything is hidden. If everything is going to come into full transparency, full awakening, it must be done in the place where the submersion is occurring. Where everyone is asleep."

"This makes me feel uncomfortable, I need some time to myself to think it over." I walked away to get some space as the events consumed me.

"There is no privacy. Don't you understand? You can walk over there and I can still hear your mind. It is not with my ears that I hear. As I see you on your approach I can see your thoughts backwards and forwards through time. You can't remove me, or hide from me, I am not a parasite. What you should instead consider is why you feel a need to hide and not just do your ruminations in shameless view of one and all. Your embarrassment prevents your freedom. You are not listening to me."

"It's not that, it's just I don't want to be pressured to make a choice for you, I need my choice to come from my feelings, not from your request."

"Why can you not feel yourself in front of me? You choose to hide as a lizard under a rock."

"I . . . I . . . don't know I am just not comfortable." I didn't know and I couldn't explain it, but it was true I didn't want him near me while I was thinking, I didn't like it. I couldn't feel myself in his presence, it was taking up all my space.

"Yes. You can hear it right? You can't see that your discomfort is only shame at your own truth. It's . . . disgusting," he said, flaring his nostrils. My cheeks flushed.

"Jeez, yea well, what the fuck, you see why I don't want to think in front of you with all your judgment?" I helplessly attempted to justify myself.

"There, was that so hard? A pinch of righteousness against a target will get you back on track right away."

"Listen, quit it with the psychoanalysis, I am not a rat in your maze. Just leave me alone for a minute, ok?"

"Fine, it's just a waste of time though." As he said those words, a scorpion scuttled into my viscera. Weird thing to say. Talking to him made me feel like I didn't even exist or matter. But I didn't want to pursue any thoughts at all about that feeling, I just tried to focus on feeling it. If I thought about it, he was going to know, he was going to know what I think. He knew everything and I hated it.

I had to focus really hard on having no thoughts at all. Instead of taking time to think about things, I tried to feel that feeling in my gut. Maybe if I didn't have any thoughts he wouldn't be able to track me. I tried to just sit and feel my body. I decided to sit down. I tried to feel the gravity pressing my legs to the ground, feel my spine shooting up into my skull, feel my breath. I kept feeling my sinews, I couldn't shake the feeling inside them and tried to go further into it. I was nauseous and constricted into one big cramp. Feeling the pain kept my mind off thinking at least. He approached me.

"Interesting," he said as his feet cleared the distance. **"It looks as though you have not been thinking."** He squinted his eyes at me and looked over my shoulder in an absent-minded manner. It reminded me of when the coyote was looking at me after I saw his parasite. Dammit stop thinking!

"Perhaps you are finally learning something," he said in a backhanded insult that I picked up immediately.

"You don't seem very fond of humanity," I said honestly, finally observing a truth about him in the gap created by my lack of thinking.

"**That is an accurate observation.**"

"Why not?"

"**Your incessant questions provide an answer to your own question.**" He reminded me of a kid in my high school that used to bully me, he was super smart and everyone hated him for it.

"It must bother you that you need me for something," I said, laughing inside. For the first time, I had the upper hand. "It must bother you that you cannot do this yourself and you need a lowly, annoying, irritating human to help you," I finished, digging the knife in.

"**Yes, it does.**" His shoulders dropped slightly. "**Everything has limits. All things in the universe do not exist in a vacuum, I have many needs, regardless of my perspective and position, you needn't gloat. I** need **you to dream for me now. If you choose to view that as a petty validation of power that is your choice, not reality.**" I tried to just ignore him.

"I can't sleep here, I mean I pragmatically can't sleep here, it won't work. I need . . . somewhere more comfortable. I also need it to be dark, those are my needs, I have needs too," I said, assured in my boundary.

"**That isn't possible. It must be in this location, due to a time space factor that I can not explain to you because you will not understand and it will take too much time.**" I could never win with him, it was always his way and he couldn't explain why.

"I don't trust you." I found myself spurting out in a confession.

"**At least you are finally coming into honesty instead of hiding. That is not surprising to me, none of you humans trust anything. You constantly undermine and throw each other to the wolves with your suspicions, your paranoias, your delusions of enemies, it's so tiring. I don't care that you don't trust me because it is not a human capacity, in general, to trust. Only a few, rare individuals have a stable firmament, the rest are tossed out to sea in ships with no anchors. You do not need to trust anyone if you just start** paying attention to and perceiving reality properly, you are all so codependent on some other thing to tell you the truth instead of simply having the truth yourself. Truth and trust are not things someone else can give to you. I am no threat to you if you know yourself. If you truly have power, then there is no need to fear me."

"Well, ok say I agree to do it, but how do you propose getting me to go to sleep here, I can't just make that happen. I can't just like, sleep whenever I want to."

"You talk of sleep as though it is a thing separated from yourself. You have no control at all, no wonder you still fall under the sway of sleep. Who decides to pee? Is it you? Or do you wet the bed? Who makes you sleep? If it isn't you who is making you do things, who is doing the things you do?"

"Well not exactly, I mean I can decide to pee , but also I'm pee shy and can't pee in front of other people. But anyway, my body decides to pee, not me." I paused for a moment there, something didn't make sense somehow.

"Oh so it's you *and* your body is it? They are separate different things? Your body isn't *you* then, according to you."

"Well yes and no."

"Uh huh."

"I mean I am my body, but it has its own thing, I don't tell it what to do. I don't beat my heart either."

"Who does? Who beats your heart?"

"My body."

"Which again isn't you. You are split into so many things. The underworld is a schism. You are split into fragments that are not true, there is you and there is your body. You and your body are one. Everything is one, your split is why you sleep."

"What are you anyway?" I asked automatically as the thought entered my mind it was out of my mouth.

"What are you? How about I just ask you questions about yourself that you already know the answer to? Let's see how long you can do what you are asking me to do." I saw a crack in him now. His impatience was revealing something hidden underneath.

"There is nothing revealed, I am as I have been for all time. It is you who is having a crack in your mental ability, and probably just from being around me. Now, lay down and listen to my instructions." I lay down without thinking. Damnit.

"Thank you. Now listen carefully, don't ask questions, if you wait until I'm finished speaking you can just follow the instructions and need not answer any questions. You must enter into the car with the person who invites you, in your dream, even though you will not want to. Go with them to the room they take you to, in the room you must get the book and join the beginning, middle and end of the book."

"What the fuck? You are telling me to do what I already did, I mean that's how you got here."

"Yes, exactly, you must repeat this process in the underworld, in order to bring me through there. You are the one who has figured this out, so you must do it, I must be able to join the levels or the underworld will remain full of death-filled schismatized souls."

"Wow, no pressure or anything," I sneered sarcastically.

"The parasite has left an impression upon you. You sound the same way it does, you talk like it talks." I got quiet for a moment.

"Ok, and then what?" I said reluctantly.

"Once you are there and you have the attention of as many as you can gather, you must get the book and open it. You must open me into the dream realm."

"Why? What will that do?"

"No one has been able to get me in there because they can't even get me out of the book. I am out now so you must do this. I need you to do this. Penetrate your memory into the dream realm. Remember while you are within the dream. You must also, conversely, bring your dream life into your waking state. This must be undertaken to close the circle, as you did in the book, now you

must close the pages of the under and over worlds so that they overlap. When the waking and the dreaming worlds are fully connected, the great awakening will occur. When you can dream while awake this is a unification on a grand scale. Once the wall is removed it will be forever broken through, there will be no more separation between the conscious and subconscious minds and humanity will evolve into full sentience as they were meant to do. The sleepwalkers shall awaken. When the waking world comes into full lucidity within the illusion, awareness shall feel the will of one and all. For one human to do this, all humans will feel it because you are all connected, then it will spread and free the Earth."
I couldn't really say anything. I just felt tired, exhausted. I really did want to sleep now. I laughed. I wasn't even going to begin to try and make sense of everything he just said. What choice did I have? Do I ignore the black hole man? Do I do what he says and annihilate the entire world as we know it? What would you do?

"Ok whatever," I said to him and I closed my eyes, trying to forget. Trying to forget he was there, trying to forget who I was, trying to forget everything. Trying to just breathe and be still. He told me to remember, but I fell asleep by forgetting.

The Dawn

The transition was abrupt. The dream came on like diving into a pool of water. I looked around. I was in a building, a school, in a hallway. I was sitting on the floor and several people were standing over me. About five others. We were all having a conversation. One of them started to leave, a young man. I didn't know him, he was about mid-twenties. His body turned to leave and I watched him go. As I looked at him, I became acutely aware that his face was still directed towards us, but his body was walking the other direction. At that moment, on a razor's edge, I realized I was dreaming. I perceived it so deeply and so completely that my entire consciousness was aware that this was a dream. Lucid and raw, I have never felt so safe and assured, so confident, like being high. I looked directly at his backwards turned face and I said;

"Hey, why are your eyes still looking at us while you are walking away?" I giggled. Because I knew why. It was because this was a dream. I asked him the question to try to wake him up to that fact, the jig was up and I was the only one in on it. He stopped and his body turned to match his face. He stood still where he was. Everyone else turned to look at him.

He walked over and sat down next to me. Several others joined us. Some guy who seemed to be my partner, although I did not know him, turned away and left, he saw something and he was going to go investigate. There was a girl sitting next to me. I recognized her, her name was Genevieve. I gazed into her face as I concentrated. So real, so real, but nothing could stop me from knowing now that it was a dream, fearlessness took my hand.

"You guys, you guys! We are all dreaming right now, this is a dream, this is a dream, don't you know that?" I pleaded with them to wake up and become aware as I had done. I could feel that they were real people, whose bodies were somewhere, were sleeping somewhere, that I could connect the two together somehow. If it was a dream, I could do the impossible, at my own command. They were all looking at me in disbelief, I had to provide some evidence. I saw a sunbeam pouring in through a window and headed towards it. I looked out the window but couldn't see the Sun, there was just a ray of light coming from nowhere.

"Look, watch, I will show you that we are all dreaming." I placed my hand into the ray, the light danced on my fingertips while the rest of me remained in the muted indoor lighting.

I thought in my mind; *smoke, come out of my fingertips*. It did. Everyone gasped

"She's right!" They shouted.

"Let me try!" said Genevieve and she came over to the sunbeam, placing her hand in it. Bubbles spewed forth from her fingers, everyone rang out laughter like the caws of a murder of crows.

"Hey everyone, watch this!" I said. My mind had a thought; *make wings grow*. Out of my back extended two resplendent and mighty wings.

I can fly now, I thought. I imagined myself flapping my wings to and fro and they followed suit where my mind led them as I initiated a clumsy ascent into the sky. I crashed into the building wall and flew down the hall to the amazement of all of them, making my way through the long locker lined hallways. I lilted gracefully down and was on foot again, the walls began to change and morph in oscillations.

As I was walking through the hall I could hear voices. There were plants everywhere, house plants dripping from the ceilings. Vines were growing on the walls and sprawling across the floors. I was in a house now. There was plastic sheeting and plexiglass walls separating different parts of the house. The space was sectioned off into a strange maze, the vines were like walls making separations between the rooms and crawling up the ceiling .

I saw through the glass in layers upon layers and there were others there, other people, watching tv, doing laundry, someone was cooking a meal. A few rooms ahead I saw someone squeeze through one of the panels into an unprotected area. They froze in place. There was a huge tiger stalking them. I couldn't tell if I was on the right side of the barrier or not, I was wondering if I would meet the same fate. The tiger had the poor fellow locked in its gaze and was crouching towards them. In a few seconds the giant cat took a single leap and shredded the person to bits before my eyes with its claws. The tiger was playing with them, mostly, it didn't seem interested in eating them or anything, it just kept scratching at the flesh like it was a toy. I noticed many other humongous felines I hadn't caught sight of before and realized I was surrounded. The only thing separating us was sheets of thin plastic.

My heart caught in my throat at the peril and I sank out of the lucidity for a moment, the dream surrounded me in its impending reality. What if I wasn't dreaming? What if I was in real danger? I suddenly remembered I could fly so I would not be in any danger. This realization comforted me and I let go of the fear. I ascended to a place out of reach and looked for an exit. I saw a door that caught my eye and landed back on the floor. There was a sign on the wall next to it that read "Theater." I was drawn in and opened the door. I entered the theater and canvassed the scene. The stage was empty and the spotlight was shining off to the corner, there was no one there. Huge windows lined the room looking out to the city outside. I gazed out of the glass to my left and could see something far away in the sky getting closer. Birds? I could not make out what it was. I couldn't take my eyes off it, by the time I had taken a couple of breaths it was almost upon me. Swarms of creatures were swiftly approaching. There were many of them, I got away from the window and ducked under one of the chairs.

"Shit," I mumbled to myself. I drank in as much air as I could and turned to hoarfrost, silent and still, trying to become invisible. A thousand shattering shards poured into the building from all sides as something hurdled into the theater. I looked up from my crouching place, terrified. There was a full group of people on the stage now that hadn't been there before. They were rushing towards their assailants. I looked around. Tigers. It was tigers. Tigers had fallen from the sky and broken in through the windows. There was blood everywhere, at first I couldn't tell where it was coming from and I thought I might be bleeding too, there was so much glass. It was coming from the tigers, the tigers were bleeding from crashing through the glass. The people, whoever they were, tried to kill all the beautiful creatures. I attempted to focus on their faces, but everytime I did all I could see was a blur. Fuzzy faces formed their facades as they rushed to meet the giant cats who were intently gazing upon them. They were shooting fire arrows at them, trying to incinerate them. Immediately, instead of trying to help the people I sided with the beasts. I ran to them as they were burning.

"Stop," I shouted, "Why Are you doing this? Leave them alone!" I somehow knew they didn't need to kill the tigers, the people were evil and the tigers were the righteous ones. I went to one of the felines that was on fire and began patting them to put the fire out. The other burning tigers sensed that I was on their side and walked over to me to get the same service like I was a bird cleaning the teeth of the crocodiles. They were docile with me, I pet them gently to extinguish all the flames. The people were just watching me trying to figure out what I was doing. When I was finished the tigers were all blackened and singed and lay at my feet, they had transformed into black panthers and were purring, just laying around. Their wounds had stopped bleeding and

I sat in one of the theater chairs as if it were my throne and I was the queen of the panthers. The people looked at me and I spoke to them;

"You see, this is all your fear. You create your own enemy from your own fear. All you needed to do was help them and they become your ally not your nemesis. The most fearsome foe may be turned this way if only you are able to see what it needs and assist it, like removing a thorn from a lion's paw. All of this is unnecessary." I turned and left the theater, opening the door and releasing the panthers out into the hall of the school. I saw two double doors that seemed to lead outside and dramatically flew out with the panthers running free after me. I flapped up onto the roof and found a place to perch. I sharply drew a breath, a sword from its scabbard, I could feel the heat from the Sun. I looked around in the sky but there was no Sun, even though I could feel its light. That's weird, I thought, wondering where the Sun went. I flew back down and my partner came out to greet me. He seemed upset, I could tell by his face.

"Why were you talking to that guy back there, what's going on?" he asked. I thought he was jealous so I tried to explain.

"He was looking backwards! Didn't you see his face?" I reflected.

"No, what are you talking about?"

"Look at my wings!! We are dreaming, we are dreaming!!! Wake up! Wake up! We can all wake up! We can do whatever we want right now!!" his face turned pale as all the blood rushed out of it and he looked around, befuddled. The others were all trying to do impossible things too and he caught on. I screamed at everyone more urgently.

"We are all dreaming right now!! Do anything you can think of, anything you have ever dreamed of!! It will work now! It will all work now! Do it now!" I looked back at him and he stared into my eyes and smiled. He raised his hands to his face, he took the index fingers of both hands and his thumb and made a box shape with them over his left eye. He looked at me through the box, and he began to shapeshift. He turned into bright colors emerging blue and white and he changed into a creature, I could see that his mind had dropped its inhibition.

He turned into a birdish entity but still had his face and then morphed again into a bright purple blob that changed into a feline beast. We held hands together and we walked, I with my wings and he, evolving into endless forms of animals, rotating freely as a breeze. We turned and looked around and everyone else was lying motionless on the ground. They had all fallen asleep.

"Shit!" I screamed "They couldn't hold it, we've lost them!! Wake up Wake up!" I shouted impotently into their slumbering bodies. I watched them all fall into the Earth, sinking into the mud. Their breathing was slow and methodical. As I peered into them I saw a brief glimpse of something moving beneath their skin, something wriggling, like a larvae in a cocoon. We were the only ones left standing. A car pulled up in front of us as it drove across the lawn. I am not making this happen, I thought to myself. I could initiate action in the lucidity of the dream world, but there were also things that I could not control. If it wasn't me who is making other things occur, who was it? I thought to myself wrapped within the slumber. My discernment touched something then, briefly, fleeting, a tease, an answer somewhere far away, a response that yes, there was something there, bigger than me that was thinking too, my mind was here, thinking, dreaming and another presence was dreaming, and thinking. There was a hint of a larger entity dreaming me within this dream and it was big, it was a feeling that my mind could not comprehend. I was struggling now to think, I was walking through tar. As I hovered there for a moment, I saw the true nature of the dream world. It was being dreamed by an ineffable being. Something that contained all of our dreams within it. A greater thing, no one else could see this thing because they all thought their dreams were their own. I felt like throwing up. I saw it all in a deep betrayal of all I had known to be true. Much like the parasite contributing to my thoughts I saw that even as intimate as my own dreams were, they did not belong to me. They belonged to this . . . this thing, whatever it was that we were all riding within. A mother, pregnant with all of us and we were just its fetuses, listening to its stories it read to us whether we liked it or not, that's what dreams were. I felt trapped and consumed by this feeling and wanted only to be myself, to have my own thoughts, my own dreams. I didn't want to dream its dreams. I wanted to separate from it and rend it from me. It felt me trying to separate from it and became angry.

"How dare you!" Was the voice I heard, the words pierced me like a million knives and I fell to my knees. "Who is the you dreaming, fool, it is only me. You will do as you're told and nothing more." I could not overcome it, it was too powerful, I had no choice but to surrender to its force. I was a small thing, a no-thing, it was the thing, not me. I couldn't find myself within it. Its presence dominated everything. I was lost. I was a component. I was a cog in its tremendous clock. I didn't like the feeling and only wanted to escape. I heard laughter echoing throughout my mind that wasn't mine.

The car slammed on the brakes in front of us, lurching me out of the moment. I looked to the side to notice my partner too had succumbed and had fallen to the ground, now deep asleep. I let out a whimper of despair and quietly knelt beside him. The driver of the car threw door open and shouted at me;

"Get in! Get in!" The car was gyrating and did not look safe. I got in anyway. The driver was . . . not very safe seeming either. When I looked in the front seat, all I could see was a pile of hair and teeth. I was trying to search for a face or some eyes, but I didn't have much luck. Tendrils of hair were gripping the wheel rolling the car over the earth like a boat plunging through the sea. Everything was wet and sticky and slow even though the car seemed to be going very fast. I tried to look out the window, but when I focused my eyes the wind blew all over them and I couldn't see. A song began to play on the radio, I was urging my ears to make it out. It should have been familiar but I couldn't recognize any notes, it was just, noise. The driver flipped its hair a bit and I caught a glimpse of some distinguishing features hidden underneath, it looked like Animal from the muppet show. I quickly looked down at my own lap and tried not to think about anything. I could see through my legs, they were . . . they were getting thin, the skin that is. I could see the vessels beneath, the pulse of my heart, I tried to lift my head up and look around and the car was gone. I looked down and I was sitting in the grass.

"How did that happen?" I mused as I got myself up and brushed myself off. I took in my surroundings and I was in front of a house. I walked over to the path and headed for the door.

My hand touched the handle to open it and go inside and a sharp tug crept up my back, I turned around to see who was there. I opened my eyes and jerked my head. My mouth wrenched open, taking in more air than it could handle. The light was piercing my wide open eyes through the sheer force of it. It was as if someone had thrown me into an electric fence. I looked around and tried to remember what had happened, the events of the last few moments were quickly fading from my memory, running from my mind, a herd of gazelles. I was forgetting everything, where I was, what had happened, who I was.

I woke with a start, winds whistling within my wretched wrinkly mind. I was not on the cliff side where I had been laid to sleep by Asher. My body jolted as I heard his voice;

"Easy now, slowly." My hands were propping me up and the damp grass was woven within my fingers, I felt the vibrations of the sound of his throat reverberating in the ground. I looked around. I was in the middle of a huge grassy field surrounded by woods and enveloped by a fence. How did I get to the grass? The green field was covered with white flowers shooting up, resembling spears from the earth. There were several right next to me, the grass kissed my fingertips, I smelled the air, I looked into the center of a flower seeing the fuzzy softness of the white petals that spread out in a hexagonal formation.

"Those are Asphodels," Asher said, reading my thoughts.

"Where, where am I? Am I awake? Is this still a dream?" I couldn't help asking because I was so very confused. I forgot I wasn't allowed to ask questions.

"Yes and no." He laughed eerily.

"Did you move me while I was sleeping?" I asked, I could swear I was being tricked. Something didn't feel right.

"No, you woke up somewhere else," he answered.

"What? That's not . . . It doesn't work that way. You go to sleep and you wake up in the same place," I protested, feeling very solid in my statement.

"But you go somewhere else when you dream, correct? Were you on the cliff just now in your dream? You have no idea what you are talking about. You wake up somewhere else in dreams and depending on the location, this is possible in the upper world as well. Perhaps you should do some reading about electrons." I hated that he couldn't just say something that made sense.

"Where are we?" I demanded.

"Somewhere else," he answered evasively.

"What?" I pretended I didn't hear him.

"Well, we could be somewhen else, but it is a loci, nonetheless," he elaborated.

"What the fuck are you talking about?" Everything he said sounded like he was speaking in some other language.

"Sometimes when you break through the levels you go through time space in different ways. It is time and space after all, not one or the other, they are intertwined. Anyway, I can't explain everything to you because you are too far behind, as I have said, it would take years for you to catch up, we just have to keep going."

"You mean we really are here right now? I'm not still sleeping?"

"That is mostly true, but you are still in the underworld."

"What?"

"I mean you still have quite a few layers to rise through. Think of it as if it is an electron going through energy levels in an atom."

"What do you mean layers? Get out of where?" I couldn't fathom what that even meant.

"We can't stop now anyway, so none of your questions matter, they are irrelevant. Please stop."

"You mean we are stuck here?"

"Only if we don't keep going."

"Goddamnit Asher! What in the fuck! How can you not let me ask questions and then just casually trap me in time space! This is so abusive! This is what traumatizes people!"

"You would be more traumatized had you stayed in the parasitic sludge of sleep you were in. You have no idea what you are talking about, you want to be the victim so badly."

"What? I *am* a victim! A victim of you and your fucked up plot."

"Oh really? You want so desperately to have someone to blame, or someone to be hurting you, for some Shakespearean drama where you are the one that falls prey. You never once stop to think I am your savior do you. It's really annoying and I need to ask you to knock it off with the crocodile tears. That's enough. Quiet. I mean it, no more."

"Who do you think you are?"

"It is tragic you cannot see that you are the one disrespecting me and then you are angry I am not accepting it. You need to choose to have faith and trust in me rather than constant suspicion and waiting to fault me for anything you like. Stop trying to fault me and trust what I am talking about."

"How am I supposed to trust you? You keep placing me in danger!"

"You were already in danger far worse than this, I am getting you out of danger. I wish you could see this. I understand you cannot see this, but I will ask you to understand my lack of patience and inability to bring you to my state of existence. That is all I am asking. Do whatever you want." My head hurt, he was taking my brain and running it through a washing machine. It happened every time he spoke. I would never win. There was nothing I could do but listen to what he said. I hated this. I hated him.

"I hate you," I said, he could tell I was thinking it anyway so why hide it?

"You don't hate me, you can't even see me, you don't even know who I am. What you hate is the loss of control and you are projecting your discomfort onto me. It's very toxic. It's quite childish and irresponsible, please stop it. Someday perhaps you will be able to control the impulse. Stop wasting time, we have to get you back to sleep. You did not make it to the book."

"They all fell asleep, I couldn't wake them up, I was the only one who was awake, I couldn't get them up. There were others there. It was working, I was waking some of them up, they saw, they could tell. There was a girl I had seen before. Some man, he was my boyfriend? But I don't have a boyfriend. Anyway, I woke them up but they fell back asleep. I forgot about the book, or I never saw one, I was with someone in a car and then I was going to go into a house. I made it into the car, so that's something."

"You need to get the book. You need to get the book. You need to get the book. There, maybe now you won't forget. Ignore them. Ignore it all and follow my instructions. Get the book. I don't know what stopped you but you need to open the book, just like you did before. You need to fall back asleep now. Go to sleep." I was tired of arguing. I hated him ordering me around. I looked around at the field, the wind was playing across the tips of the blades of grass and making them move in waves. Wherever we were it sure was pretty. I was just going to pretend he wasn't there for a while. Try and ignore him. Try and forget. I lay down on my back, I could smell the cold damp Earth beneath me and took a few zephyr breaths in and out. I really was relaxed.

I could feel the grass, feel the breeze blowing gently across my face. The Sun danced upon my skin. Then the feeling of hot water running over my hands was so strong, I looked down. I hadn't seen any water there before, how did my hands get in the water?

Mnemento Mori

I dropped my gaze and the water was gone. I was at a house, in front of a door. My hand was on a door knob. I walked in. Strange feeling, I had been there before but the place didn't look familiar. It smelled weird. It smelled moldy. It was damp and chilly, the cold ran across my skin. I could feel things with my senses here. I tried to concentrate on the smell and the feeling of the cold. How could it be so real? I walked into the kitchen over to the sink and it was full of dishes. I just picked them up and washed them automatically. I reached over, my actions were purposeful, I had done it before but couldn't recall. I was making coffee. I heard a voice behind me;

"Can you make me some too, babe?" I looked behind me. It was my ex, he was sitting at the table reading a comic book. My stomach sank when I saw him, rage and resistance filled me in a swelling tide.

"Get it yourself!" I shouted back at him. I hate that guy! I thought to myself. Why am I with him? I asked, the thought drifted in a reverberation and wouldn't leave. I hate him, I repeated over and over again. Where am I? The thought dramatically injected into me. I looked around. This place is not familiar. Where is this? I could remember *him*, the memory of him pulled me back into remembering. I drifted off looking at the wall. There was a picture hung, it was slightly askew. Black bamboo wood framed an image of a tiger standing in the grass, it was looking right into my eyes, I could see the tips of the grass blowing in the wind. The face of a panther peeked out from behind the tiger and I was funneled into the room in the house I had been before. Been here before, the walls were plexiglass again, there was a tiger prowling on the other side, I had dreamt this before, it all spilled back into my mind in a waterfall and the tiger in the picture frame caught on fire.

I stopped dead in my tracks. Wait a minute, what is this? My mind walked through a cobweb. A gossamer wisp just beyond my grasp. I said out loud as though I was making an announcement;

"I don't live here!" Lucidity plunged into me like a knife, deep in my bones as my knowingness heightened to a crisp edge of attention akin to standing on the top of a very tall building. A hyper-attention gripped me and everything was simple and uncomplicated. There was no confusion at all as I entered into a state of steady calm precision. The certainty that I was dreaming released my confusion of everything else. As long as I knew one thing, I knew everything. I spun around and looked right into his eyes.

"You aren't real! We broke up, you can't fool me, you are dead to me, I would never be here," I screamed at the thing, whatever it was. I saw his eyes flash yellow and there was another layer beneath, behind his eyes. Something moved behind his eyes. His skull seemed hollow, transparent. I looked closer and it was wiggling beneath the surface of its skin, making it appear as a latex mask cheaply and thinly covering over a wolverine. The same thing I had seen in the others in the first dream. Something about this place was not as it seems.

"What are you talking about, can I have some coffee or what?" he demanded, clinging to the facade which made me more secure in the truth. He was lying, there was no hiding the lie.

"I know you aren't here because I hate you. I would never be with you. I don't choose this! I didn't choose you, you aren't here! You are dead! This is over!" I shouted in a shrill commanding tone, I was trying to convince him of the truth I already held, I was more saying it for myself.

"Who are you!? Show me your face!!" I stomped my foot hard on the floor and I saw his skin droop a bit. It had slipped slightly from the force of my step.

"Aha!" I yelled and ran towards him like a missile to a target. He stood up quickly and now his demeanor had changed, he could not pretend anymore, I saw through his disguise. He slipped free from the costume. Shivering and writhing under the false skin I saw it start to rip and shred around the form. A pale, sickly skin emerged from beneath and produced sparse thin hair all over it like a boar. It had bright yellow glowing cat eyes that were almond shaped.

"Who are you?" I yelled after it as it turned, ignoring me completely. It climbed the stairs. I alighted the staircase, it was walking up and I stopped to find I couldn't move any further. I watched as each time it took a step the space above it engorged, see through and transparent. It was fading away. As I perceived this disappearing act, I looked up into where it was going and the ceiling disappeared and turned into outer space. When I saw it a surge of electricity coursed through my body. I had seen it before, I had seen it when I was awake. I looked back down into the room, it was still intact, still the same. There was a bookshelf in there. I looked back up at the being ascending the stairs who was levitating now, into some black hole in the ceiling. Asher! The name screamed in my mind.

"You need to get the book!" The voice echoed and I was pulling a memory like a thread out of my mind, it was looped together with the ex, the past, this house this time, everything bounced back upon itself, a superball trapped in a cube. I was hanging in mid-air, suspended. I looked down at the living room. There was a bookcase, I ignored the abominable whatever it was and shifted my focus. The light intensified, brighter in the room resembling a Sun rise over the couch, laser rays emanating everywhere. The room was so jagged, I heard every sound my feet made as they touched the floor. Hyperfocus consumed me, every rustle of my clothes was a symphony. I breathed in on purpose, reached down, and grabbed a book from the shelf. It didn't really matter what book I chose, because all books were all books. I looked down. It was the bible. I held it in my hand staring at it, noticing everything, feeling the weight of it in my hand. I had it, I had the book.

When my line of sight cleared I saw a table and chairs where the thing had been sitting before, pretending to be something it wasn't and I went over to sit down and opened the book. I pulled out the chair, but before I could sit down I saw something out of the periphery of my eye. There in the corner of the room, lit up for all to see was a brain. A rather large brain at that. The brain-ness of it was unmistakable, its pink snake coils arranged in the symmetry and purpose that any creature could recognize. I looked around, back towards the door, up towards the staircase, expecting at any moment for the owner of the organ to come furiously barging through in a lobotomous lunge and claim it back. The brain was leaking some sort of phlegmy liquid, bundling it in a slimy, fishy coat. When I looked closely at it, there was a throbbing, or pulsing in a rhythmic movement, which if the idea weren't insane, I would swear was breathing.

I could not tear my eyes from it, and as I stared at it, I could see that it had an intention of entering me. Some memory floated up through my mind of a hitchhiker such as this and I felt very distraught. I could almost see it trying to force its way into my head in a parasitic plan of a horrible hermit crab. I looked down and upon inspection, several slimy tentacles protruding from the bottom of the brain were now wrapped around my foot, squirming as a squid. Beyond my control, a girlish squeal parted my lips and I ran round in circles several times trying to dislodge the octopus, till I tripped and landed in a skid. The tentacles, closing in tighter, were odd, I squinted and saw eyes at the tip of each wormy end. Snakes! I tried to grab them with my hand.

But I fucked up, I looked at my hand. My hand was so weird. I couldn't get over it. My fingers looked like the snakes I was trying to grab and I couldn't tell which was which, they all writhed together as a pit of vermin. I could see the veins in my hand, they were snakes too. I saw the blood pumping through the veins of the palm of my hand moving in snakey rivers. I couldn't look away, I forgot about the book and stared harder into my hand, into the brain. The blood in my eye matched the rhythm of the blood in my hand, the blood in the brain. They were beating the same, all I could see and hear now was a pulse, a beat, a boom. BOOM! It was so loud. I was rudely thrust up out of sleep and into consciousness as though there were a giant hand that reached down and pulled me out of a river.

I was awake. That was it. I had awared myself right out of the dream because I couldn't get over feeling my body, seeing it for what it was, this odd thing that was holding me.

"**Damn,**" I heard Asher say. My eyes opened and I tried to lift up my head. I couldn't move. I attempted to look around but there was so much dust it hurt. Sand everywhere. My whole body had pressure on top of it, I was stuck.

"**Try not to move,**" Asher said calmly, almost whispering. No shit, Sherlock, I wanted to say but held myself back. I could hear the wind and it was hot. We must be in the desert. Fuck. I was under a rock. Great.

"**It's going to be more difficult now, you don't get it. Every time you fail you have to work twice as hard to not let it take you. It wants you to follow it instead of following yourself. It wants to take you, it wants you to sleep. Think about it, it's winning, you can't even see. What happens when you sleep, have you ever even tried to stay awake? It is unraveling your focus by taking it away from you. You must stop forgetting, stop letting it take you.**"

"No, why would I ever try to stay awake, what are you talking about?" I answered, trying not to open my mouth very wide to make sure no sand got in. I already had a mouthful of it, grinding in my teeth obnoxiously.

"**Exactly. Why do you think that is? It doesn't matter. You couldn't fight it if you tried. It would still take you, regardless.**"

"What would take me?"

"**Sleep. You fool. Sleep. You cannot keep it away. Always it will win, it will take you as though a hand was pulling you into the ocean to drown, you can't stay on top of it.**" The wind died down and I could open my eyes to take in the view. I could have been on another planet for all I knew. The red sand formed dune hills as far as I could see into the distance. We were at the foot of a rocky mountain and I had somehow managed to wedge myself into a crevasse. I had so many questions, but I held my tongue because those would not get me anywhere but a mouth full of sand. I had to go bigger, had to try and see the larger view. I pulled air into my lungs, tilting my head away from the sand and just thought about everything he had just said. It was true, I mean I hadn't ever really thought about not sleeping because it was just what everyone did, sleep. You had to sleep, that's just how it was. We all slept.

"**Stop letting it tempt you to go off task. In the dream, the same thing is happening to you that happens when you are awake and you fall asleep. You must hold on to your discernment in the dream for dear life, you must fight it. Don't fall into the dream and let it take you. Don't fall asleep, slap yourself in the face. You have to focus, you have to concentrate. Don't get distracted. You need to know as you go in now, it will try and not let you get it. It is going to try and stop you from getting the book now. You are no match for it. All you have to do is remember, you must use your memory, it is your only chance. You must not let your memory of your task fade no matter what happens, do not get caught up in the illusion of the dream. Just as you have no control of your life direction, you have no control of your dream direction, until you take that control of your memory.**" I didn't understand what he was talking about but he was just going to make me keep doing this until I did what he needed. I strayed then wondering if this was all my life would be now, maybe there would be no return to something after this. Maybe this was it now, everything was going to be something else now and I couldn't just finish this and then go back to being regular. I tried to alter my attitude from fighting him to trying to integrate what he was saying, I tried to breathe deeply and soften, and relax.

"Ok, so I have to just remember, while falling asleep and through the dream to get the book, that's it right? So, how do I do that? How do you hold a memory? Is there a trick or something? You are just saying "remember" like it's no big deal, but obviously it's a huge deal, so is there some kind of device or technique I can use that will help me remember so I don't have to keep doing this over and over again?"

"I didn't want to do this, but I have no choice. I realize it is only going to feed your pity story but I can't deal with that now. It's too bad. The only way you humans seem to be able to hold a memory is your own pain and the fear that you will have pain again. Your pain prevents the release, I don't know why, but it does. For you, pain is a vault."

"Wait what? What are you talking about? What are . . ." I stopped. He looked evil, he had shifted. His eyes disappeared and were replaced, my bowels shuddered and constricted. For the first time, there was malice palpably emanating from him. I was trapped under the rock so there was nothing I could do. He slowly approached me and I could hear an audible ringing in my ears that thundered louder with each step he took. My heart pounded and everything was coated with blue light. He lunged at me and grabbed my arm, hard and purposeful. I couldn't break his grip, I tried to wriggle free but there was nowhere to go.

"No!" I screamed in desperation trying to look him in the eyes, but I couldn't find him, he wasn't there. A small seizure spread sending shreds inside my sinews

"Stop, be still," he said, his voice was different. He lifted his hand towards my face and the hand he was pressing into my arm slid down in a fluid motion. My arm was instantly on fire. It felt like I had just been lashed with a whip. I didn't want to look but I had to. I turned my head to peer down at the damage. Blood was pulsing into the sand. I was paralyzed by the pain and I wept unabashedly. I wanted to scream but I couldn't make any sounds come out and just lay there with my face in a suspended shout.

"**Now you will remember,**" he whispered deeply into my face as he backed away and readjusted himself. "**Now you will remember, you will not forget. Get the book, open the book.**" My mouth hung open, useless as my face contorted. I tried to focus on my breathing and the throbbing rhythm of piercing distress. The fluid frantically flowed, filling forgotten foramens. The pulsing pain from the blood blindly bounding into the sand filled my eyes with red.

"How the fuck am I supposed to go to sleep now?" I whimpered into the sand, sobbing.

"**Be quiet please.**"

"Am I going to be ok? I think you really hurt me really bad. Am I going to die?" I said, searching for some glimmer of compassion. I couldn't tell how much my arm hurt and how much pain was because he had done this to me. What if he was actually trying to kill me to get into the underworld? The underworld was the place for the dead. I remembered very acutely that I could die doing what he asked and I could not get that thought out of my mind after it entered. There was that tug, that scent, almost out of reach. Someone else is dreaming me, someone else is living me, something . . . something dying for me. It was dancing at the edge of my periphery but I couldn't rope it in.

"**Be quiet please,**" he repeated coldly. "**Go to sleep.**"

The Awakened

I lay there shivering. I could feel the hot wet blood pulsing out of my arm at a steady pace. The boom, the same boom from my dream. I was remembering it from before but it was happening again now. It was fake, a copycat, a mimic. I saw the blood pulse in my eye, everything was shaking with my heart beat. The boom, the pulse. I was pulsing everywhere. I could feel it everywhere now, I could feel it in my feet, my feet were pulsing. It mounted and amplified, I could only breath and pulse and breathe and pulse. I could feel my toes pulsing, my feet were a throb.

I looked at my feet. They were running. The memory of the boom had brought me back. I didn't remember falling asleep. I went to sleep by remembering this time, instead of by forgetting. Was I even asleep? It was getting hard to tell anymore. I was running, dripping blood, I looked down at my arm, I was still bleeding. I almost came out of the dream, it was slipping away, I was myself again, waking up. I caught a hot feeling of being underneath the rock in the desert for a brief flash, but then I saw something that sunk me back down into it. Wait, that's not my arm, it was the arm of a man. I was a man. I had no shirt on, I had big muscles, I could feel my strength. I was a man, I was inside a man but I was still me. I was running through a swampy forest, my feet didn't even have any shoes on, running barefoot. The sweat was dripping down my chest. I had been running for a while, but I didn't feel tired. I was . . . strong. I saw the blood on my arm and thought book, book, book.

I had no idea where I was headed, I just kept running, mechanically, breathing in, stepping, breathing in, stepping. I heard rustling behind me, a sound in the brush. I was being followed. Shit. I didn't know there was going to be danger. I panicked, what if I got hurt here and it bled into reality as the wound on my arm. What if I died here? Could I bleed to death in a dream? Maybe all the people who croaked in their sleep passed away in a dream and were trapped in the underworld forever. I looked around wildly, more desperate now.

I saw a clearing through the trees up ahead and bolted for it as fast as I could. I was spat out on a beach. Shit, no cover. I was out in the wide open. Had to hide. Had to hide quickly. I jumped back into the brush and kept running parallel to the beach. I could hear them getting closer. They knew where I was, where I was going. Something was up ahead. It was a wooden shack, some kind of structure. Is that the dumbest thing ever to go in, I thought to myself. They would have to know I was in there, still, I had to go. I couldn't run forever even if this was a dream. I looked at my arm again, book, book, book I repeated to myself, but I stopped, what book? I could feel my memory slipping away, being carried down a river. I kept having to catch it if I didn't keep it with me, keep it present, I would become completely lost in where I was, even though I wasn't even really there.

I ran up to the shed, I was breathing so hard I thought my lungs would burst free from my chest and flap around in the sand. The old shed was weathered by the Sun and beach, it had turned a kind of grayish color and appeared it would crumble to a pile of dust if a wind blew on it. Huh, the Sun, I remembered to look up into the sky, I couldn't find the Sun. There was no Sun. I took careful steps because I remembered getting a splinter in such a place when I was a child . . . Oh no . . . I had been here before, wait had I been here before? A labyrinth of fog clouded everything. My memory flooded with thoughts in a relentless pounding storm. I was overtaken by a tidal wave. I was a child now, running through the sand to the shed, I had no shoes on. It was windy.

A sharp pain struck my foot and I didn't understand what was happening, I was confused and scared and crying. Now I was in a basement, it was cold and dark I was standing at a freezer, I was a child I was screaming and crying I looked down at my foot, there was a bee, I was grabbing a popsicle from the freezer and I had gotten stung by a bee on my toe, the prick of a splinter, wait splinter? It was slipping away, I could only feel the sting. As my memory of the time unfolded in my mind, I was there, teleporting from world to world. I couldn't swim back into the man, I was trying to hold onto him, hold onto where I was, or had been but I was being pulled apart into another place. The splinter had split me back into a memory of when I had a similar pain, when I felt pain in the same place, the same location. I took my thumb and drove it savagely into the wound on my arm.

"Ahhhh!" I screamed out and the sound of the voice was not my own as instantly I was the man again, hearing his voice. My thumb buried deeply into the flesh of my arm. Book, book, book I repeated to myself as I panted.

"He's over there!" I heard a shout to my left and swung my head around. They had arrived. There were two of them. One of them was holding a woman by the neck who looked barely alive. She pleaded into my eyes with pain and memory, a familiarity of the body I was in. She was bonded to him. The man holding her was fat and sweaty, wearing overalls. He had a straw hat on. Hicks, I thought to myself. The other one was heading towards me. He wore a black hat and a trench coat. He was sweating and breathing hard, holding a shotgun. I tried to get as much information as I could with my eyeballs and wondered if somewhere Angela's body still existed with her eyes closed, that I was trapped inside of. I peered as deep as I could into the men holding my wife. I saw the wriggle beneath their skin. Something about the people in this place, there was a being beneath the surface, but I didn't know what it was. Shit. I got up and ran to the door. I wrenched it open, the wood had rotted together with the frame. I kicked it shut behind me. No lock, not even a door knob. There was a huge anchor in the corner and I managed to shove it across the floor to block the door. The two men were laughing outside.

"Haha nowhere to go now, Jake, you may as well come on out of there," one of them hissed.

"That's fine Henry, he can listen through the walls while we shoot his wife," the other one hissed. I heard her scream. I looked around the shed, not much to work with. An old chair was turned over, covered in bird shit where they had made a nest that was now abandoned. There was a pile of trash in the corner, branches, papers, something under there, I went over and started to dig through it. A book, there was a book. Book, book, book I repeated to myself as I grabbed it.

BOOM! The sound cracked so loud I jumped out of my skin. I peeked through the paneling of the poorly structured wooden walls. The two men were standing over her, lumped down in the sand. They had blown a hole clean through her, I could see her back, torn out into her chest. Her ribs spread out like spider legs. The boom made me pulse, I could see my pulse in my eye again and I was tugged, unraveling, being drawn out, getting thin. I was remembering the boom, but my recollection was a muddy marsh and thick, I was swimming through honey now. A shriek entered my ears and pulled me back into it. There was a woman there now, right beside me in the shed. I stood there staring at her with the book in my hand, she was a transparent ghost.

It was her, my "wife" or whatever. She was here in the shed. The men were throwing themselves up against the door now while she solidified, more and more opaque, apertures adjusting on a camera. It looked fake, a projection. Book, book book, I kept thinking.

"Jake! Why didn't you save me Jake! I trusted you Jake! I loved you!" My wife shouted filled with despair. Her form began to quake and shatter. Her mouth dilated supernaturally long, in ways it shouldn't have.

Spikes were emerging from the sides of her body, ripping through her clothes. They bristled out and bent, snapping and cracking. She was expanding to fill most of the shed. Her legs sprouted hair on them and moved independently, she crawled up the wall into a corner

"Jake!" The spider thing called, it was going to fucking attack me, what in the actual fuck. The absurdity and insanity of the event kept trying to pull me out, my mind could see it was a dream but I couldn't stop looking, it was too weird, I was completely hypnotized, I was watching a movie and I could not blink my eyes. That's it I thought to myself, blink your eyes. Do something, take charge, shape the dream. I purposefully did a hard blink.

BOOM! I was knocked over from the force of the blow of the shotgun blasting a hole clean through the door and the opposite wall, I could see through to the ocean. The memory of the sound ricocheted through my body that was throbbing from my arms, throbbing from the splinters that were now lodged in my naked belly. I was disintegrating again, I could feel the feeling, now familiar and blinked my eyes again, harder this time. The book, the book, the book I had to force my mind there, I sat on the floor, understanding it was just going to keep happening. I had to stop paying attention to it, to the spider wife, to the men with the gun. Ignore it, focus, concentrate. I blinked again.

I saw how life was much like this, a dream trying to trap you in its drama, in its intrigue. It was all a trap. Everything was a ghost spider wife's web you couldn't get out of. The entrapments of life were meant to steal your focus from discovering what you were there to do. I had to get the book, I had to ignore the spider woman, I had to ignore the danger and that was the most insane choice I could have possibly made, for anyone to make such a choice in living reality they would have to be completely mad. I understood now that there were reasons behind these seemingly deranged decisions that the many would never know, because they would never come into this perspective and begin to comprehend the inwardly driving forces, the inner motivations, some actions seemed so foreign to them. Some measures seemed so dangerous to them only because they did not appreciate the larger scope of what those undertakings were for. When you do not grasp larger things, you will never do certain actions, and that will prevent you from becoming larger, from becoming great.

I sat there on the floor and I placed the book in my lap, calmly, carefully. My resolve was set and nothing could pull me from it now. I didn't give a fuck what these crazy fuckers did, I had something to do and I was going to do it. The men were screaming as they saw the spider woman and they were falling over each other trying to escape but a web shot out of her body chasing after them through the hole in the wall and pulled them towards her in a nightmarish tangle. One of her legs reached over towards me pinning my leg to the floor. I could feel it so strongly, it was so real, I laughed, so real. I ignored it. Carefully and purposefully I took the first half of the book in one hand and the second half of the book in my other and bent them towards each other to make the heart. I had won, I beat it. I beat the dream. I kept holding the pages in place, nothing was happening, just wait I told myself, wait don't stop. Hold it. Hold fast.

A cool caress brushed my cheek. It was the wind. I shut my eyes in deep relief. I had done it. It was done. I had no idea what it was I had done, but it was done. A tornado cycled in circles inside the shed. The wind picked up and wailed forcefully. Dirt dust and sand were flying everywhere and the door completely ripped off its hinges. A figure materialized in front of me. It was quiet, silent and swift. It was soft and smooth. He was there, it was him, but he was not himself, he was a woman. I could tell it was still Asher, I could *feel* him, but he was there, a woman, a beautiful woman. She was wearing my clothes. The same clothes Asher had worn. What the fuck was happening. My skin crawled as the recollection of Angela inserted itself into me. Asher looks like me, but I didn't think that. Asher resembled Angela, was the thought I had. I was not Angela anymore and Asher was Angela. But I was not Asher, I was some random dude. Some guy named Jake apparently.

"Asher! Asher! I did it!" I called his name out to him. Did he not see me? Could he see me? I mean she. She passed by, she kept walking. She just kept on walking. Time stopped, ceased its eternal immortal movement just for me, to swallow me whole in the moment and rip my organs from out of my body to spill their contents onto the floor with a dull, lifeless splat, just because she could. Her feet were touching the floor of the shed, but not really, everything was melting around them. Overlays cloaked upon each other, erupting into visibility as I was unraveling again, disintegrating again, disappearing. All I could see was her back as she began to fade away.

Her frame filled the horizon. My heart ached. I was unloved, invisible, unknown. A stranger. And that was it, Asher was gone. I was left here, trapped in the dream world all fucked up. My injury wasn't disappearing, it didn't vanish. The only thing disappearing was the dream world around Asher's feet. My wound was still there, it hurt. I had just done God knows what. What was I supposed to do now? What was going to happen? Hopelessness shadowed my face in a dreary crow. I had to keep it together, prepare, I was going to need to keep my head on straight. Remember, I had to just keep remembering. Dreamember, I thought to myself. I had to dreamember. I had to keep my feet rooted in what had happened to me, keep rooted in my memory. My thoughts assaulted me like thugs. I had to completely disengage my need to know, to question and focus on what was occurring. I couldn't even do that. Everything was evaporating, the men were gone, no spider wife, no shed, no sand. I was smooshed in static, a place of no being.

What a fool. I was ashamed, stupid for trusting him. I had followed all the instructions, I had passed all the tests. But how could you really feel stupid, I argued with myself. He fucking fell out of the ceiling in your hotel room! Of course you don't argue with people who fall from the ceiling! Even though I logically understood this it was clear I had been completely manipulated and strung along. All I wanted to do was be useful.

The Betrayal

The image of Asher walking out of my life into the dream world, the underworld, wherever this location existed, was already beginning to fade. I was on a boat rowing further and further away from a shore being swallowed in mist. Location, the word kept repeating in my mind. Location. I was somewhere, wasn't I. This is some kind of location. My mind wandered to how I kept waking up in different places when Asher was trying to get me to the book, different locations. Where was this location? I am somewhere. Where am I now?

"So what happens now? Where am I going to?" I heard the far off voice of the parasite singing to me, a memory of a moment like a dead friend. I couldn't tell where I was any more. Looking down at my body, I was still him, Jake or whatever. I was definitely not back in reality, whatever that meant. I was a man now, and Asher was a woman, was me? But it was not me. A strange thought to see that we could be deposited into any random body but remain ourselves, or that someone else could occupy our body that we had come to know as ourselves.

I looked around, the dream world was mutating rapidly. I gazed into the sunless sky and watched it contort. The backdrop looked like water pouring over a drawing and the ink was starting to run. The interstitial matter was shaking now, making small vibrations I could just barely see, the world was blurring into a swamp. I could make out something behind it, moving backwards through the cracks of an overlay. The waves were growing in size, shaking free what had been trapped within. A faint blue light was glowing everywhere. I looked to the skyline as the structure dropped, the underworld was removing its dress. I could see a grid forming, it was red squares on black, outlined in the way an old LED display on a clock formed. The sky was a hazy misty sapphire color without any stars, contrasted by a vast red matrix that seemed to spread out into infinity. It was empty, I couldn't see anyone or anything, just me. I was all alone, in the center of some kind of video game version of daynight. I reached out my hand and tried to touch the grid, but it just slipped through, insubstantial.

"Fuuuuuuck," I said out loud. I could be imprisoned here forever and I had no idea what was happening in the overworld, or if that even existed anymore. I could be inside a bible for all I knew. Was that it? Had I been tricked into replacing Asher within their prison, folded into some page somewhere? Maybe they were parading around as me in the real world. I drew in a sharp breath, whoa, I didn't even know if the world was still there or not. I don't know what I had thought was going to happen if I helped Asher, I guessed I would get some kind of reward, was I that shallow? What a fool. Asher could have been Satan or something nefarious, I really had no clue what or who Asher was. I mean who would expect Lucifer to pop out of a motel bible? As though the bible was a secret Ouija board.

I could see now how stupid I was. How could I have been so wrong? All I could do was follow life and go along. Just go along . . . shhh shhh shhh, my mind's eye traveled to the memory of riding my bicycle, the wheels turning as they were pushed in circles down the street. Follow along, the phrase kept repeating in my mind getting louder and louder each time. I *had* just been going along and following. A melee of memories marched through my mind. I spontaneously saw myself from a different angle entirely. Someone else's eyes were placed inside my skull. I was outside myself looking down on my body, being led along a path, stepping into foot steps already laid out in front of me. I tried to remember the last time I had made a decision, made an actual choice, made a life for myself. Who left these tracks? It had not been me. Who was trying to trick me into going this way, taking advantage of my lack of attention? I had no control which was why I had ended up everywhere, perhaps there was a different way. I sat down as my life swirled around me, an angry swarm of hornets. I was just drifting through, floating along, being carried on a current, a bloated corpse. What did I choose? What is my choice? The question rang maddeningly in my brain. The lucidity was coming on, I was forced up through layers of sleep, eons of time. I could sense the thing dreaming me again, felt it wrapping around me like a python.

That's when it happened, I woke up within my waking dream. I went another layer in, as if someone tore off hundreds of pieces of clothing from my body. Something had cut into my cocoon, and the web was all unraveling. I could . . . remember Jake and who he was, what his life was. I remembered my now dead wife. Jake had been real, or at least real in the dream world. It was all unfurling within my mind, petals on a blooming rose. He had been born, lived a life, did things. I felt queasy as I saw that this could be true for everyone with the dreamed realities that they were "real" in a way. Maybe not real but there was something behind them.

Jake's memories merged in my mind, shoving themselves into me, it hurt. Jake was waking up while still trapped inside of my awareness that was running through his now occupied body. I clutched my head with my hands as it waved over me, fighting the integration, trying as hard as I could to hold on to Angela. Angela, Angela, Angela, I kept repeating the name. I tore one of the hands off my head and placed it on the wound in my arm. I pressed into it with my thumb. Angela, Angela, Angela. I tried to focus, tired to fight off the data invading me. I tried to think of all the memories I had that were mine. I wasn't even Angela anymore, I was another thing. I was trying to find an anchor to what and who I was.

Something ripped, a tear in the fabric. My mind split in two. I was there, clutching my arm in the underworld, holding on for dear life to Angela, whoever that was now, trying to ignore the life of Jake, whoever he had been and stood on two feet that seemed to belong to someone else. Then I found myself, there between them both. Somewhere I had arrived. The one who was holding them, Jake and Angela, it was me, someone was there, I could feel myself. I was wrestling them, there was someone there, someone doing the wrestling. That someone was me. I was aware of what was happening, directing the ship, guiding the journey. I fell into this new me. An unfamiliar presence, pure and raw.

I am here now. This is a dream, now. Where was this dream world living really, in whose mind? Whose dream is this? I thought violently. This is a dream, this is a dream. Who is dreaming? The grid shivered when my mind found that question and locked onto it. I was in a dream that something was dreaming. The knowing of that single thing brought me peace.

"I can do anything, I can do anything." I kept repeating it over and over again. I needed to stop thinking about Asher, stop looking at them and focus on myself. I needed to understand my power, my boat in this river. So what, maybe I had been taken advantage of, I didn't need to remain frozen. There was no need to dwell in the place of astonishment at what I didn't know. I had to move forward with what I did know. Let's look at the bright side, my mind told itself. I am here in the underworld, in the dream realm. I can do whatever I want. I have power here, more than in the other place whatever that was, wherever that was. I had to stay where I was and look at what I had to work with.

"Be here now," I said out loud with a chortle. I was abandoned by Asher, but I can still do whatever I want. I fell into spasmodic fits of heaving laughter. I was only sad because I was perceiving some kind of loss instead of seeing what I had been given and what I could do. That was it, that's what it meant! It was so stupid I could hardly believe it. The middle of the book, the psalm, it was "be here now." The message of the middle, between the two lines. Time, it was talking about time. The reason it says eternity in the middle was a riddle. Beginning middle and end were about time. How do you get to the middle of time?

I can go to Asher at any time! I can go wherever I want! I kept thinking within my mind, I can go wherever I want! The lucidity was mounting as the walls of my thoughts crumbled and became fluid.

"Take me to Asher!" I shouted out loud, I voiced it as though I were an empress making a demand. And then, I was there. I blinked and everything changed. A wink of my eyes, and as my eyelids rose, the scenery altered. I didn't even have a sensation of movement. When I fell asleep into the underworld, it was a tug, a pull or a drop, this was different. There was no sensation, just a moment passing through the eye of a needle. There was Asher, I could see her, she was beautiful. I was far enough away that I didn't think she saw me there yet, I had to make sure to not feel or think anything, she would sense me if my mind made even the slightest vibration. I tried to just breathe, empty inside. She looked like Angela, at least I thought she did, but maybe I was projecting. I wasn't really sure how I used to look, I had forgotten.

She was speaking to a crowd of people in a field. The grass was long, up to everyone's waist. The people were as flowers growing in a meadow, I remembered the smell of the asphodels. She was standing up on a hill and talking to them all. There were hundreds of people. They were all transfixed by her, I could feel them listening. They hadn't listened to me that way. No one paid attention to me when I tried to tell them to wake up. Why were they lending an ear to her when she was copying me? In my body! I could feel the rage and jealousy welling inside my heart. I wanted to destroy her. This wasn't fair. How could someone else be more successful than me in my own body, it really pierced me. My internal organs began producing some kind of liquid vitriol that was a new kind of substance than I was familiar with. I wanted to murder Asher. How dare they? I felt robbed of my very being, the only thing I truly owned, my face. It was wearing my face, doing the things I could not do.

"I hate you," I whispered under my breath. Her eyes turned sharply and looked right at me. Shit. I had no idea what I was going to do, but it was too late to think about that now, I just had to keep going. Asher launched into a levitation with her hands down at her sides, she rose slowly into the air, making a dramatic display of herself.

"Good grief," I said out loud, rolling my eyes, I wasn't afraid of them anymore. She hovered over the crowd who all reacted as though it were a miracle, she was Jesus as far as they were concerned and they were all oohing and awing.

"I can fly too," I said, "All of you can, stop staring at her, she isn't special. You can fly too, don't be stupid," I shouted as loudly as I could. I could sense them, they didn't want to be powerful. They felt more comfortable watching Asher be powerful than doing it themselves. Asher came ever so slowly, enjoying the reaction of the crowd, and gently lowered herself to the ground. She said nothing, and waited for them to gather, to make sure she had an audience. Everything felt staged and fake. I couldn't hold myself back anymore, I looked Asher in my eyes and let my spleen come up through my mouth in my words.

"How could you do this to me? I thought you cared about me, I thought we were a team? You stole my skin! What are you?" I shouted.

"I am not responsible for your thoughts and I can see you are still inside your narrative. You are focused on me, I am not focused on you. Why would you think I was doing all this to you at all? Fool, this is for the world, for all humans, how can you be so small as to make what I am doing about only yourself? Can your vision truly be so limited? Ask yourself, why are you making me about you?" Asher said as the crowd nodded in agreement at every word, lapping it up in gluttonous gulps.

"You are wearing my body you psychopath! How am I making this about me when you are literally parading around as me! You stole me from myself, I can't believe I even need to explain this to you! You could have at least told me what you were doing or said goodbye! Done anything to show we were friends at all," I begged.

"Why is any of this about you? What does it matter what I look like, or what you look like, what does that have to do with anything?"

"I am the one here, I'm talking, it's me, that's what it has to do with me, I am here, I am doing the talking right now. I need to be included or it hurts, you treat me as though I don't exist," I protested.

"Why do you need me to prove your existence? It seems you are giving me more power than I deserve. I certainly don't need your validation to know myself. I know exactly who I am," Asher retorted.

"Who you are is in my body!" I screamed again, outraged at the lack of acknowledgement. "I need you to see that, to see me, so that it doesn't hurt me so badly! I thought we would do it together, you could have had some thought of me," I pleaded.

"Your thoughts are incorrect. You would only get in the way, and it would take too much time for me to explain. I did what I had to for the greater good and that's all that matters, you can lick your wounds somewhere else," Asher bellowed, refusing to give any ground.

My heart sank. I just didn't care anymore. It was clear Asher gave not a shit about me at all or anything I would ever do. I was invisible even while they were dressed in my flesh. The string my heart held for him snapped and twanged out of tune. All Asher cared about was accomplishing whatever it was they were going to accomplish. The internal decision to take action was an urgency that was new for me. I had always submitted to circumstance, been accommodating. I didn't even hesitate now, I was not going to follow along. I was going to do what I wanted. All I could feel was my rage and desperation to show Asher how selfish they were, how they had completely disregarded me.

I began to grow. Not like where they talk about growing your inner child, I mean I was fastly getting larger, Alice in wonderland larger, after she ate the caterpillar's mushroom. The feeling of wrath overcame me. I was uncontrollably expanding. It was an unstoppable physical reality, a convulsion, a sneeze, an orgasm. I was possessed by my body, Jake's body and nothing I did could stop it from its completion. Once growth from a realization begins, there is nothing you can do to stop it from reaching its culmination, the inevitable consequence of physics, as certain as death. I saw the grass growing smaller and I was shooting up into the sunless, sapphire sky. Asher was a gnome standing below me now, my rage had puffed me up into a peacock tail that fanned out around me. I had unfolded from somewhere inside of myself. I was the origami, I didn't need any pages to fold me. The crowd gasped and withdrew in fear, Asher seemed dismayed that they might think I was more powerful so tried to match me and imitated an inflation, lest they lose their adulation.

Asher was straining and pulsing, swelling into a balloon. It wasn't as good as mine though, I could tell she didn't have the emotion behind it and was forcing it through. The people seemed confused at the display, but were watching expectantly. As Asher rose up before everyone, she noticeably expanded in size. Toad warts bulged out of every inch of its corporal shape in all directions, she didn't look good, which gave me some pleasure.

"You summoned me Angela. You did this. This is your fault." Asher was still trying to insult me, I was bored.

"Pfffft," I snorted, "you inserted yourself and I was naive. This is all about you. You can't pin this on me. Nice try," I volleyed.

"How do you think it is possible that any of this is happening? Do you think that you just enlarged, was that you, do you think you did that? How do you think I came out of the book? You think it was a fluke? A one off? Did I make that happen, or that it was from your doing? You are so ignorant it is painful to me, you are unable to see the bigger picture," Asher stung, I could feel the mind fuck coming on.

"I mean, I don't know, did some kind of sorcerer trap you in there like a Genii in a bottle?" I joked.

"So you don't think a spirit could be contained in other forms of matter? I know you are feeling the truth that you are inside of something already. Maybe you think you put yourself here, that you are some omnipotent being that does not exist within another more powerful thing than yourself. Astounding, how could I not recognize your 'power.' Truly I am the fool, not you," Asher said without blinking in a way that made my spine shiver. Oh no, I could feel the truth of it. I could feel that this wasn't me. there was some other me inside of me. The other me made me very uncomfortable. The way the parasite had been in me, but I was feeling me in me, I was the parasite.

"Fool, you think books are the only things that can unfold? You yourself are enfolded within your body. If you could see your spirit that has been folded into your flesh, you might think twice about what you just said. But you can not, so you are ignorant and blind. You are in there, your real you is a diamond shoved into a rock. But look at how you need me to tell you this because you do not know it yourself. Pathetic." I could not speak, I just listened. The crowd was silent. Hanging on her every word. I imagined barfing all over them and I thought it would be funny.

"I'm not here for another one of your lectures where you know everything and you try to teach me something," I answered, placing my hand on Jake's hip.

"Trust me I wish I didn't have to keep pointing out the obvious to you," Asher teased. "I know that you are feeling a different you within your form that has nothing to do with your body. What you are feeling is the thing that is creased into the material world. There is something folded inside you. You know what I am saying is true and has nothing to do with any of your perceptions about me. The truth does not belong to you or me, it simply is," Asher intoned. I really didn't want to bother talking to them anymore. I had released the sense of intrigue where I wanted to figure them out like a puzzle. Asher didn't care about my disinterest and continued giving their sermon regardless, probably excited to have an opportunity to impress their followers.

"**As soon as they are done with you they toss you aside, see how the apathy for anything other than self is shown in them?**" Asher shouted to the crowd, pointing to me. "**This self interest will cause all the harm, all the violence in the world. It will cause all truth to be denied in the name of the self. They will never think of the other. Until we reach the gem folded into us all in order that it awakens we are doomed to be trapped within self fulfilling prophecies and death. You all have something folded within you, please do not ignore it for your petty battles with egos.**" The people were enraptured, mesmerized by Asher's lies. They shifted underneath their skin. I saw it now, what was beneath them. Their eyes all glowed yellow, like the thing I saw in the house. I saw the sparse hair as they shed the frame of their facades. A group of naked ape-like creatures with glowing golden eyes stood in the place where I thought there had been people. Were these people? It was like a sasquatch. Was that what people really looked like? What is this, what are we? I couldn't focus on them any more. Maybe they only looked like this because they still had parasites in the overworld, preventing them from being who they were supposed to be. I couldn't focus on them, I had to keep going.

"But the whole reason I'm here talking to you now is because you disregarded me! You thought only of yourself and not of me! I am here telling you how selfish you are! You are such a hypocrite!" I squealed, my voice cracking from the pain.

"**You are wrong. I am doing this for everyone, it has nothing to do with me. You just think it's me because the person, the self, the ego is all you can see because that's how you are yourself. You can't see what's folded inside me anymore than you could see me in the book, in the bible before I emerged. You couldn't see your own parasite because all you can perceive is the smallest part of yourself. I am so much more than what you behold. Your inability to have a relationship with anyone or anything is because you** can only see yourself and that blocks your entire view. You can't **unfold until you see everything as you truly are."** The weird ape people all nodded their heads in agreement, convinced that Asher was actually here for them and not trying to take control and power in any way they could. That really stung because I didn't have relationships, I didn't understand other people. I didn't have any friends. But it wasn't because of what Asher was saying, it was because people betrayed me and I didn't want to engage with painful things so I just left all the time. The only person who had even helped me recently was the coyote, and look at what happened from my accepting someone's assistance.

"I'll try to explain this to you on your level," Asher said condescendingly as the ears of the many perked up, interested in collecting the words like dew on the flowers at dawn. **"How bad do you feel when you break up with a romantic partner,"** Asher asked me, swiftly changing the subject, feeling my thoughts about the coyote.

"What? Um it depends," I answered nervously.

"It depends on what?" Asher demanded.

"Depends on if I loved them," I answered matter of factly.

"Why do you love them and not others?" Asher pressed on.

"I don't know, you just love some people," I answered.

"Why not love all, why only some."

"I don't know, that's just how it works."

"Well you are wrong. you can and need to love all things, regardless of your own preferences. That is how you become less selfish."

"Don't you think that's a little unrealistic?" I posited. It was too late now, I was playing along again, they had hooked me again. Ugh, I was so disappointed in myself.

"I think it's unrealistic for you to withhold love from anything, especially as a kind of punishment based on your perception or judgment, and not even considering everything else that person has or will ever do."

"What?" I was flabbergasted.

"What gives you the right to withhold love, it does not belong to you to pick and choose. Humans are so arrogant and you call it free will, you are really just assholes. Humans are so arrogant they have made themselves smaller than they should be due to greed, it's your own fault. You like me, now you hate me then it is all dependent on what I do or how you view me. Trust me, you know nothing about what love really is, and you give and take it and think that you should decide whether or not I can have it. I cannot stress how passionately violent that is to me and you. Angela, you are the criminal here though you pose yourself as the virtuous saint of love who gives and takes it as you please. I am never without love, ever, and you can not take that from me."

Asher was growing quickly now. The emotion had broken through. I pissed them off, that gave me at least a little satisfaction to see some kind of effect I had on them. The crowd was scattering. It was time to leave. I had no idea what Asher could do, I needed to make an exit. I don't know how I knew what to do, no one told me, I hadn't even asked. The knowledge of it had arrived, a boat sailing through the water, it just showed up, right there, right when I needed it. I had to fall asleep. I had to fall asleep inside the dream. I might have once thought it impossible to fall asleep there in the middle of such an obviously dramatic situation. Comparable to falling asleep while you were being eaten by a tiger on fire I might imagine. It had to be done. I closed my eyes and thought to myself;

"I order you to sleep!" The thought bounced inside me like light ricocheting off a mirror into infinity. The pull sank in and I was down. I surrendered without any resistance. There was a slight tug as my body hit the floor. I heard a song playing in the distance, it seemed far away. I was already levels deep as I fell through the realms. I was falling in slow motion through blackness, through nothing. A soft feeling broke my fall and I was laying down somewhere, the pressure of the mattress pushed against my body. I was asleep in a bed, but I didn't know where and I couldn't tell who I was. What body was I in? It was

dark in the room. My eyes were closed and I was laying in a bed but I could see the room in the darkness with my mind. I stayed very, very still and tried to feel into my surroundings. I was in some other place, another location, another realm I had never been to before. There was a door to my left.

I heard footsteps at the door. I was frozen and I couldn't move. The doorknob turned slowly. The fear, it was so real. I became lucid from the force of the fear pushing my mind up to the forefront. My perceptions heightened to a pinpoint. I was dreaming but I wasn't sure if I could have been awake in some strange reality somewhere, I just wasn't sure. The stark reality of the horror filled me in a way that was so visceral, so brutal, I could not deny it. I could do nothing to stop it but lay there and listen. Asher and the crowd of people, the meadow had all disappeared in an instant, a blink of an eye, like I was riding some train and the scenery kept changing. My nostrils smelled adrenaline and gasoline, it smelled terrible. The door opened so slowly that time stopped and stuttered. It was a film going frame by frame. The hand, if you could call it that, on the doorknob moved into the visible spectrum after what seemed an eternity. The hand was covered in shadow, it was dark but dark in a way that was devastatingly dark like there was a black hole there. A full-on shadow figure filled the frame of the entry and I could feel it looking at me even though it didn't have any eyes. Palpable emptiness filled the space of its form. I had never felt emptiness like this before, it was upsetting , I could feel the lack of anything and I had to fight falling into it, becoming absorbed by it, by the void.

A thought entered my awareness; Gatekeeper, my mind said to me, in a voice that was my own. This was a gatekeeper. I didn't know how I knew that, but I did and it was true. It was definitely not Asher. This was something different, an attendant, a servant. It was looking at me, even though it didn't have any eyes. I could feel it penetrating me with its mind, observing me, watching me. It was trying to stop me from waking up in another location, the overworld. I knew very strongly that it wanted me to stay asleep, it was trying to bury me down deeper. Was this sleep itself? It was trying to stop me from going anywhere. It was a presence of darkness that was the darkness itself, I could almost feel, it was wearing the darkness in a shroud, a cloak, a disguise. I could feel it wearing it, and I was trying to push it aside, like parting a curtain. I wanted to see what was underneath that darkness, I wanted to see it naked without its clothes, to undress it, to unfold it so that I could see the truth of what it was. I could sense the darkness wasn't real, wasn't the thing itself. It felt me pushing on it. I could feel it getting aggressive, we were mind wrestling. It didn't want me to see it, didn't want me to know it for what it was. I could not move. I pushed. It was trying to keep me down, keep me asleep.

I could see everything, a powerless observer. The thing was trying to put a dream inside me. I could sense its intentions, there was another being behind it, giving me the dream, some kind of dream giver that was masked in darkness, in shadow. I was able to ascertain it all, and it was creepy. The thing was trying to embed a dream into me like downloading a song or an anesthesiologist, I knew I had to resist it and not permit it to enter, or I would stay asleep. This felt like some kind of nurse or attendant who gave people more sedatives as they were trying to get up and I had to fight it.

It was too late, I laughed inside my mind at it because I knew I already won. I see you, I know what you are doing. You have no power over me. The shadow figure approached me. It was trying to touch me, I couldn't let it, but I couldn't move. I tried to speak, to make sound come up out of my throat but I felt like I had no body, there was nothing I could attach onto that could make noise. I couldn't connect to the body that was laying there, I could feel it all around me but it wouldn't listen to me. It wasn't listening to me. My rage began to boil in my belly.

Speak! I commanded the body, like a dog, as I had commanded myself before. *SPEAK!* A small sound came out of my mouth and the shadow froze. It stopped advancing. *Speak!* I shouted again inside my mind. A rumble resurrected raucously, I would not quit, I kept yelling.

"No." The word finally arose. The word was no. All I could say was no. "No!" I said again. "NOooooooooo." There was only a tone escaping the throat of whatever form or body I had taken, here in this place.

"No!" I shouted and broke through, I could not move the body, but I could shout. Now I was yelling, I was screaming long and hard .

"No! No! No!" The shadow ran away, it had reabsorbed all the fear it had been emitting, all the terror I had felt when it came into the door.

The scenery changed on the train ride again. I was somewhere else now. The room had vanished, the bed was gone. I had woken up, but not quite all the way I could sense. I was still somewhere in between, not quite anywhere. The shadow was gone, I had gotten through another layer. I was alone, surrounded by darkness, as though I was inside the shadow being, like I had entered into its belly. I was dressed in a golden suit, which shone so bright it mimicked the glitters of the Sun. Darkness pushed in around me, persistent and penetrating. From slightly below my belly button, the suit tore in neat zigzags making a labyrinth. My umbilicus undulated, and retched, heaving heartily till one final hurl hocked out a single, perfect eye that gazed back at me, lovingly. The light emanating from the luster of my suit was diverted, reflected and focused through the eye, sending the light in a precise laser beam wherever I Imagined it to go. I spoke a word of command and the eye closed. I shouted it again and the weapon opened anew, ready for action. I laughed uproariously, in a rhythmical beat, which settled into a droning drum, pulsing, then pounding the meat of my head. Everywhere the eye focused rainbow beams of light pushed their way through the dark around it, illuminating all the corners with prisms of sparkles. Whatever this deep shadow place was that I had found myself within, I could understand that all it needed was something to see it in order for it to shift. I did have a presence here, just like the darkness did. Both of us were here and I could affect things too. I didn't need to just lay there and be influenced, I also could take action.

"Take me home," I announced out loud and understood the steering wheel of my ship again in silent lucidity. It wasn't the dream that was the entry into the underworld, it was the subconscious, you had to get there by dreaming because you entered your subconscious in the dream. The dream was only the boat, the vehicle to take you there. It was impossible to enter this part of mind while awake. It could only be done while dreaming, as though some lock or system had been put on the mind of every living creature. I had just solved the game. I did it. I found the door. The gateway was just being able to descend into another part of mind, of embodiment, of . . . there it was again, that fleeting tug towards an almost tangible grasp and then it quickly retreated into the shadows. By resisting a dream being given to me I was able to enter my own subconscious mind, to see the wheel of the ship and become the captain. The shadow force was my subconscious, or not mine, but *the* subconscious. I had to see it, even though I couldn't see it, I had to look at it. That's what the gatekeeper was, the darkness itself.

I propelled past the threshold, shredding the barrier, I was falling through the darkness again. I fell for hours and landed with a hard thud on a carpeted floor. I looked around. Impossible. How could this be? I was back in the fucking hotel room. There is no way anywhere else in the entire universe could have had those elephant paintings. I exhaled in deep relief, I never thought I could be so happy to see such horrendous art. I melted into the shag, I wanted to kiss it, but I could still smell my puke somewhere. Thank you thank you thank you, I was so grateful to be back in the world, this sliver of familiarity was so grounding. The bag with all my old clothes in it was still there on the floor, I riffled through it and threw some of them on. How long had I been gone? What day is this? I wondered, I had completely lost all of space time somehow. It hadn't been that long or someone would have come in to clean up the room, I had not arrived before any of this happened because all my things were here. My things, Angela's things. Angela. Memories came back into me as I thought and said the name, I remembered who she was. It was a specific feeling, like an old friend, it didn't really connect me to her again, it just kind of made me sad. I was so grateful to know that she had been real, had been here, her clothes were evidence, I had proof, I had to wear these to help me remember, help me hold onto this feeling of her, this knowing of who I had been. I breathed in deeply with my nose buried in the clothes to memorize the smell, her smell, my smell.

It didn't last long. I heard a violent crash on the street and jumped up to peek out of the curtains like a fugitive.

It was nighttime. Cars were ramming into each other all over the place, there was smoke and fire, chaos erupted like a volcano everywhere my eyes wandered. What was this, was I still dreaming? Panic enveloped me. There were some bodies strewn about and birds everywhere, so many birds. I looked closely to see they were mostly crows, but also eagles and hawks, no songbirds, only raptors and carrion feeders. Some of them were flying into each other, they were engaged in a melee to devour the flesh that was so messily spread across the streets. It was pouring down rain. The water was making everything shine, making the streetlights create halos around all the scenes dramatically, like a spot light of rainbows. Reflections were bouncing off of everywhere, doubling the images into each other. The wet street made a reflection of what was above, like an island mirrored in a still sea. I saw my face reflected back to me in the window, I caught the gaze that was gazing and saw everything was a reflection upon something else, intangible, illusory. I felt the looker and the looked upon, enmeshed into a single mind. I was still Jake. I instantly felt the disappointment sink into my heart. This was my new prison. I looked at the mirror of glass. How could glass be transparent and reflective at the same time, I did not understand. How could an image be on the other side, and also this side, superimposed upon each other in translucent layers. So strange, to look into another's eyes that were mine but not mine. My eyes were layered upon the eyes I saw, my mind's eye could see but in a glass reflection, much like the window I was looking through with another's view. I felt like I was borrowing a form, not in it. I had a brief possession in my memory of a time that had passed where I was Angela and I was looking at my face while putting on my make up in the club. I couldn't connect to anything, to any face. Faces were interchangeable masks that were replaceable, what was looking through the flesh? I saw light hitting my eyes, Jake's eyes in the window but they felt lifeless to me. I remembered looking at the eyes of a fish I caught when I was child. I had left the fish on the beach for a while as I kept pressing my luck to catch another, discarding what I had already caught, seeking the new. When I returned to my trophy, it had turned all grey. There was no sheen on its eyes. The glossy finish the water had provided all dripped away into the sand. The eyes of the animal were covered over in a kind of dull dress. Had this once been a living creature swimming merrily through the stream? That seemed impossible now, it was only a husk, a discarded piece of trash. I felt I was trapped inside Jake's husk now, veiled within some cloudy, fishy corpse.

I had to break away from these thoughts filling me, they had no end and no resolution. I had to turn away and look back into the room. I must have fallen through the ceiling just as Asher had. How could I fall down from below, in the underworld? I had a spatial distance challenge in my mind over trying to reckon the navigation of it all and found myself laughing because of all the impossible things I was experiencing that was where my mind was stuck, on where "down" was. Hilarious. Did Asher come from the underworld to begin with? That son of a bitch. I had to shake my head and give up following the trail of intrigue to contemplate the lies of Asher, or I would only become infuriated. No, I was not going to let that overcome me. I had to focus. I would not be able to just escape back to reality and forget all about everything that happened, I mean, I certainly couldn't as the flesh of Jake surrounding me made that impossible. The world was falling apart and I was still inside of Jake. I had to keep going, I was just going to need to commit to following this through. I knew too much, had done too much. I was thinking about how upset I was that Asher abandoned me and I knew that meant I could not do the same to myself. So many times in my life, I had given up on me just because someone else did. I had to hold on, even if everyone else threw me under the bus. I had to fix this.

THE EXORCISM

Shit. I was going to need the coyote. This was a desperate move, but it had to be him. I laughed as I understood that just because I didn't like the truth, it didn't make it any less true. He could figure it out. If anyone could figure this out, it would be a coyote, generally speaking but also, I didn't have any other options. I needed him, and I hated that I needed him. His instincts would be so helpful, plus I knew he would do it. I guess the time you find out you really need friends is when you really need them. The mirror flexed back upon me in my mind, thinking maybe that's how Asher had felt about me? That they had just needed me and then discarded me when they were through the same way I was using the coyote. I had been so angry at Asher for doing that to me, yet here I was doing the same thing to someone else. I shivered somewhere deep inside.

I had to go and find him. He would be confused and angry, I ditched him after all, but he was maybe the only person on Earth who could see the real me in this body, and I knew all the way down to my pinky toe, he wouldn't let me down. There was no way he would be able to do anything with that demon on his back though. I was going to have to get his parasite off of him, there was a lot on it. I had no idea what to do. How do you even explain to someone that they have a parasite attached to them when they can't see it? I was certain that the mental hospitals were filled with people who had made this realization and were put away for life as a result of seeing something they shouldn't have. The person trying to tell you the truth would seem completely insane, simply because you could not see what they were seeing. Now I grasped how Asher must have been tormented. It's impossible to even speak with anyone after you have been through certain things. Why even bother really, trying to articulate it. There was no way I could provide all of the data for any of this, and anyone I spoke with would have so many questions. I mean, who else could I even get to help me, how was I going to explain this to someone? I would be confronted with questions forever that were useless until, whoever it was, went through the process, came into understanding. No amount of inquiry would replace the experiences I had been through. Useless, language was so . . . useless in many ways. I didn't even know where he was. I just had to hope he would be there, the strip club. Ugh.

I couldn't believe I had to go back there after everything I had been through. I felt like an old man trying to crawl back into a vagina, hoping to be reborn. Except I was me, a woman turned into a man in the underworld who had to go back to a job she quit to solicit a peeping Tom to capture an interdimensional being. I made the decision and pushed open the door. If reality was a comedy, it would make sense because it was like I got hit with a pie in the face. The sheer stupidity of what was occurring was all too clear as my eyes ran over the panorama of disarray before me. One thing led to another and when something occurred out of the order people were used to, their reactions to the unexpected set off a chain of events that was even worse. Maybe even bad things weren't so bad but our response to them amplified the disaster. If only humans could navigate something they had never experienced before, maybe it wouldn't have been so pronounced in its repercussions. Each tweak sent in motion a thousand others and I was bearing witness to that sad fact of physics as it spread out at my feet. A car slammed on its brakes when it saw a fire in front of it and all the cars behind just crashed into each other. A person witnessed the crash and began running in panic into other people who in turn ran into more people, mirroring the cars. The karma of consequences of actions was not spiritual mumbo jumbo, it was more like science and measurable. If this then that, was the situation of the disintegration I was currently observing. I had to disengage and come into focus. I had to stay out of the storm.

I thought about jumping in a car that had been abandoned but by the look of it, the roads weren't very safe so I decided to foot it. I still didn't have any shoes on, none of Angela's shoes fit Jake, who had been barefoot the day I entered him, so I had to just roll with it. My legs began to move, responding to my thought of the action and obeying it. It felt good to use the muscles in this body. This body loved to be moved. I remember hating exercise in Angela's body, it was always such a chore and I had to try so hard. I knew I could run the whole way, I wasn't tired. Jake was a really good runner. I had to run, because otherwise I would stop and look at them, the people. If I had my bike I could go even faster to eliminate the chance of any interactions. I guess it was still at the club, lumped in amongst the comedic costumes and thigh high boots of that stinky back room. The people paraded past me in the infectious stream of causality in cinematic revelry, but I averted my eyes. Their parasites would see me. I couldn't think about any of that or get caught up in some distraction. I had to just run. The chaos engulfing the world was apocalyptic level. the corners of my awareness were extending as though I was on psychedelic drugs, I felt like this was just a dream too because it was absolutely not following the rules of the reality I had grown accustomed to. I must still be dreaming, that was the only thing that made any sense, this was all only some dream that something much larger than myself had envisioned, I hated to admit it, but Asher had been right about that. Reality too, was still in a dream, it was just a different location, hard to wake up from. I couldn't stop to think, or look at it or I would just slip uselessly into the state of fear and paranoia that was enveloping them all. Even their parasites wouldn't be able to help them think their way out of this. I wondered what they could possibly imagine was happening and it was not weird or strange that people made up religions to explain things.

I turned my gaze up to the heavens, the Sun was gone because it was night, but that meant I could still be in the underworld, had the underworld infected reality now? I couldn't see anything, too dark and cloudy, so hard to tell. There were flocks of parasites flying through the sky, circling vultures. Perhaps their hosts had died and they were just waiting till they found someone without one. These frantic manta rays could be new ones waiting to get in and I had just never seen them before, never noticed them always there. I quickly ducked under a tree as the reality of this thought sunk in and my stomach squeezed in repulsion. Oh God, what if one got back on me. Ew ew ewewew. I had to just keep moving and go as swiftly as possible. Sometimes ignoring things was a really good option.

I slowed my pace and stalked up to the back of the club quietly. I saw all the rats and the heaps of trash, and a wave of malaise washed over me along with a small piece of comfort that even in the apocalypse, vermin and garbage remain consistent. If there was a complete opposite to fond nostalgia, I was feeling it now. The dread of acceptance maybe? My mind went into a state of attempting to reject the memories as they arose, trying to hold back the waters behind a dam. I had tried to hold so tightly to Angela's memories before, but this, I only wanted to forget. Here is why no one wants to remember and we do not seek memory. Here is why. I had been here before, been inside before, but not as me as I am now. I guess it was a good thing and meant I had learned something. When we don't want to repeat the same mistake twice, perhaps that indicated I had graduated in some way. I was there, but I wasn't, I had been there but I hadn't. My senses were on fire. The place was an abysmal pit of a thousand horrid sensations. I could feel everything inside it, I was holding onto a bag of writhing worms I couldn't let go of. I didn't have any other choice so I took a deep breath, held it in and did the walk of shame back into the club of the living dead. I was trying not to breathe so that I wouldn't smell the place, it wouldn't last very long. Eventually the stench would enter into me, permeating my membranes. I could smell the smell just from remembering it. The place itself was flooding my nose with the memory of the smell so I might as well be smelling it, I took a deep breath in defiance of my own resistance.

I opened the door and walked in. I was immediately blown back by a chaotic din of shouting, only, when I looked at everyone's mouths, no one was saying a word. I could hear their thoughts, no one was talking, it was their minds, I could hear their minds. All their thoughts, all at once and it was awful. What a mess. Everyone always thinks it would be so cool to have telepathy, to know what other people are thinking. Well, It turns out, it isn't. Everyone wants ESP, wow, let me tell you right now, when you get it you will be like please make it stop. Trust me on that one. I grasped why all the occultists turned into alcoholics, it was just to make this stop. If you ever wondered why all those wizards and witches are mean it is because they have to listen to this all day. The disappointing truth of what occupies the minds of the many is quite a wake up call. Gross.

The club had changed inside just as the outside had, nothing was normal anymore. Everything was different, you would think if one thing would be dependable, it was a strip club, but the change had penetrated even here. Instead of being a sea of swirling bodies and movement, the club was calm now, muted and quiet. The girls were all huddled together near the stage with grim looks on their faces as I went into the main room. They were all fully dressed, no one was working. Most of them were staring at the floor or nervously picking at their clothes, vaping and smoking cigarettes. Some of them were engaged in conversation with each other while their eyes darted nervously around at the empty space. There were only a few men in the club and I saw Gus off in the corner talking to the bartender as they both drank straight from booze bottles behind the counter. They were gesticulating wildly and raising their hands up in the air, shouting about something.

I could see through them, as I looked closer. I saw through their skin. I could see their blood pumping, they were translucent. I could see how the parasites were attached to them, the tendrils reached down and wrapped around their spines, up their necks hugging their skulls. I tried not to look any of their parasites in the eye. It was macabre, like observing some kind of creature in a cave for a nature documentary. I could see their eyeballs behind the lids covering them, thin as rice paper. Their clothes were on them but I could see through those too. It wasn't sexy either. Those x-ray specs they used to have in the back of comic books that formed fantasies for so many teens, if they only knew what they would see. Fleshy tissue paper draped over the scaffolding of their bones. I couldn't stop staring. I heard the sounds of their lungs breathing, scraping as the bags of skin rubbed against each other. I could see their esophaguses and the food inside them. A jumble of meat just going about their meat business.

I saw the two girls I had met in the back room, they were sitting together, eyes wide, slamming shots of whiskey. The dark one was wearing thigh high stiletto heels and some kind of cape, while the preppy cheerleader one was dressed in neon pink. They were quite a team. I could see their minds moving and thinking separately from their mouths. They were having a conversation, while thinking something other than the words they were saying at the same time.

"We should just go and snag whatever we can from some of the biggest houses in town!" The dark goth one said, in her mind I felt an image of herself as a powerful queen seated on a throne with servants attending her while she waved a scepter around a room filled with concubines. "There hasn't been any daylight for weeks now, it's not like anyone will see us."

"What if there are still people in there? Or dogs? It's still way too crazy out there, I think we should find a safe spot to hole up with some supplies and food for a while," the day glow woman answered as her

mind envisioned terrible murder scenes and bloody carnage of everyone shooting each other. "Maybe we should wait until the sun rises, it
has to happen eventually."

"You are such a killjoy, where is your sense of adventure? No one
cares, don't you get it? Who wants to hurt each other when everything
is so up in the air, they are all just going to be doing drugs or fucking
or something." She had still found the time to put on her make up and
the dark smoke around her eyes made her pupils flash and glow with
excitement. I watched her mind project scenes of sneaking around
with a truck and loading it up with jewelry, gold, cash and everything
that was the most useless for survival when all of those things lost their
value. The futile schemes of small minds.

"I'd just rather play it safe and live to see another day, you know?
Like we don't know what we will find out there. I'm just gonna go
gather some food at the store and make my way uptown to some
spot on a hill so I can see what's going on." She was seeing herself safe
and warm by a fire eating some canned soup. Pragmatic, I thought to
myself. I wondered what they meant that the Sun was gone. She said
weeks, how long had I been gone?

"Suit yourself sweetheart. Maybe we can catch up later." Her mind
was already searching the room for someone else she could pull in to
assist with her plan, only to ditch them later while she snuck out and
took everything for herself. Transparency was haunting in many ways,
at least I had felt shame at having my mind exposed, but I realized,
hearing their conversation, humans are what they are, deep down inside. I looked around the room, searching for him, bored by the reality
I was witnessing.

That's when I saw him. Bingo. Jackpot. Thank God, thank you
God, for the first time in a while, a glimmer of hope, I have never been
so happy to see a coyote in my life. He was sitting at a table in the
corner watching everyone, chain smoking from the look of the ash-
tray in front of him. His leg was twitching in nervous tension and his
mind was heavy with thoughts. I ran up to him, emanating joy and

excitement on my face. He saw me right away and threw up his hands, palms out, pushing back his chair and standing up. Oops, I forgot I wasn't me on the outside. I had grown to really enjoy this body. I was more . . . comfortable in this man-body for some reason. To be honest I was excited that I might not ever have to menstruate again. Maybe it was just the contrast, it's hard to explain. It was easier to be my true self with the loss of my old body somehow, I think it was unrelated to the gender thing. I connected to a me that had nothing to do with my body, because I was in another body. No way would I have ever gained this perspective otherwise. I had forgotten all about Angela's body being in here and was just focused on myself, on who I was. I also really liked how I could run inside of Jake. But I'm exactly and one hundred percent sure I would never be able to explain that to Willy in a million billion years. He was definitely going to miss Angela's body, and not connect to Jake's body. But if we really did have some kind of psychic connection, why would that even matter? I crossed my fingers that he would still be able to feel me, know who I was, understand and sense me. I was counting on his coyote super powers to override his pervy creepiness.

"Easy Pal, I know its wild out there but stay the fuck back I don't have anything for you. I don't want any trouble, Gus over there can show you the way out," the coyote said. He didn't recognize me at all. Dangit.

"Willy!" I shouted his name, hoping that would help, hoping he could hear me through the face, through the voice I was presenting with. His expression contorted, it was kind of cute.

"Willy, it's ok, look can we talk somewhere private for a minute? Nothing weird I promise, I know you don't know me, but I know you, and I need to talk to you," I responded, whispering, trying to attract as little attention as possible. Not like anyone would care, they were focused on other things in their daydreaming.

"What is this, who are you?" The coyote bristled, taking a defensive stance. I was trying to keep everything cool, but it was too late, I saw it and it saw me seeing it. His parasite had peeked out and I looked into its red little eyes. Ugh. The creature quickly shot back behind his spine and the coyote wretched, gagging at the sensation.

"Jesus Christ!" Willy said. He was in pain, his face curved in a way that showed the strain.

"Look, just come with me for a second, Angela sent me, ok?" I said, trying to make him believe me.

"How do you know Angela?" he shouted, getting angry and confused now, spitting as the words spewed out of him in slow lava syllables.

"Trust me, I am going to tell you all about it," I answered, grabbing him by the hand. I glanced around to make sure no one saw us, they all seemed preoccupied. The first door I saw was the men's room. Barf, are you serious? I was going to have to go to the men's room of a strip club? I mean, I guess not only did no one care because the world was falling apart outside, but I was also a man now, even though I really didn't understand what that meant. I led him in, taking a deep breath again as I figured the stench in there was going to be rank, perhaps I could spare myself a few moments of olfactory purity. The coyote's eyes widened when he understood I was taking him in there and he stiffened with fear of the unknown. Ha I thought, now you know how chicks feel getting into your car. We passed over the threshold as I practically had to drag him in there. The walls were cement, showing large patches of dampness from some unknown fluid that I hoped was water, a burst pipe maybe? There was a blinking neon light overhead giving everything a strobe effect, but I was grateful for the poor visibility and tried not to look around too much for fear of what might be lurking in there. I ran out of breath and was forced to intake the air, which proved to be just as I had suspected, dreadful. What was it about men that stunk so bad all the time, it smelled like piss and urinal cakes. And who the Hell thought of the name "cake" for something you pee on. And what did those things even do, they certainly only made things smell worse. I looked down and tried to make sure I wasn't stepping on anything and looked him in the eyes.

"Ok pal, what the Hell is going on?" The coyote demanded, and rightfully so, it was an astute question, considering.

"Willy, it's me, it's Angela." He rolled his eyes in disbelief. I guess I should have expected that. Sigh, this was going to take longer than I thought and I just had to deal with it.

"I don't know what that bitch is doing or where she went or why she thinks its ok to try and fuck with a guy's head, but you can tell her, I don't appreciate it one bit. Not one bit at all. You go give her that message for me, wherever the fuck she is," the coyote stated, it didn't bother me because I could tell by his forced tone that I had hurt his feelings, which was surprising.

"Right, I don't expect you to just believe me with no evidence, ask me whatever you want. We met here in the club, you drove me home in your car, your red DeLorean that night, you took me to the hotel with the awful elephant paintings."

"She could have told you all that, and the paintings . . . I didn't know she thought they were awful," he said woundedly.

"Ok, ok look, let's just forget all that. How about if I tell you why you keep feeling that sensation of a centipede crawling around the back of your neck."

"What?" I immediately had his full attention. His eyes went wide. "How do you know about that?" Now he looked scared more than confused. I didn't blame him.

"Why don't we start with, when was the last time a worm squirmed around your neck? Was it when you were with Angela? Have you felt it any time other than when you were with Angela? If I am not mistaken you just had a slithery snake slime around back there right now, correct?"

The coyote cleared his throat. "Yes, I did."

"I can tell you why you just wretched again right now. I can tell you."

"Why is that?" he said, speaking very purposefully now, squinting his eyes at me.

"Because, Willy, I am Angela. You first convulsed at the wriggling in your bones when I came to meet you outside the hotel room, and the reason your nasty little hitchhiker back there lost his shit was because of what happened to me in there with the otherworldly whatever it is. The thing you are feeling is a parasite that has attached itself to your neck."

"First of all, if you're Angela, why don't you look like her, what is this, invasion of the body snatchers? And second of all, you tryin' to tell me I got some kind of tapeworm?" He wasn't buying it.

"Look, you may have noticed things have happened, things have changed, I assume you came here because you didn't know what else to do because the world is being engulfed by chaos. Maybe this is the only place you hang out, I don't know anyway that's beside the point. What is going on anyway? Why hasn't the Sun been coming out?"

"What has that got to do with Angela and tapeworms?" he barked. "You probably know as much as I do since the news stopped. No one is telling us anything. I heard someone say the Earth stopped turning, but I think the rich people are finally killing us off so they can do whatever they want." I was cringing in the memories of me asking Asher endless questions and took a deep breath in. There was no way he would come up to speed with me. He was going to be so resistant to all my explanations. Lord, was it even ever possible to really communicate with each other. I needed to just demonstrate something to him, something drastic, so he would just listen to me and follow me and do what I told him to do. Words weren't working.

"**Willy!**" I shouted at him from within his own mind. I fully invaded him. I just went there and ripped myself into him. He jumped and his parasite writhed. He doubled over in pain as the feeling sent him to his knees which rested on the filthy, damp floor.

"Ungh what's happening?" he cried out. I was dripping with pity for him. But it had to be done.

"Willy, it's me Angela, we need to take your parasite out and you need to come with me back to the hotel," I mind yelled into him. He rolled around on the disgusting concrete. It was hurting him. I had to be careful, he might die. I also had to get him up off the nasty pestilence filled ground.

"Ok," he said quietly after a few moments. That was it, he just got up and walked out without any fuss at all. I understood now why Asher had been so forceful with me. Here I was losing patience with the coyote just as Asher had with me and I had made so many complaints and Willy didn't make a peep. We made our way out of the club and got in his car. The streets were growing worse, but I didn't feel like I was in any danger when he was driving for some reason. People running everywhere. Fires, water spraying. It was a hot mess. I tried not to look and just focused on my lap. Coyote didn't say a word, just calmly drove through the war going on outside like nothing was happening while he lit a cigarette. I found myself grateful for some familiarity, to have him here, to be in his car. I was soothed by the familiar presence of his car, the way it smelled of smoke. It was linking me back to Angela, I remembered how it felt to be her, to be in her sitting in this seat I was sitting in now. Coyote shifted in his seat. He could feel me remembering her. He connected to me for the first time. Bingo.

"I told you it was me," I said through Jake's mouth, since we were finally familiar.

"What on Earth is going on Angela?" he said, acknowledging my presence for the first time, continuing to swerve through the restless streets. "Is this the end of the world? Are we at the end of the world? You know something about all this, I can tell. Can you tell me?"

"Yes, I do and yes I will," I answered him respectfully. "I don't really know what or why this is all going on, but I do know some things. I know there is some kind of creature trying to change the way the world is and I know that I helped this creature. I don't know if they are good or bad, but I do know that it is too late to go back and I have to try and stop them now. I also know that I need your help to do that. If you will help me.”

“Is the creature the reason why you ditched out on me Angela?”

“Yes, it is.”

“Oh, ok. I was kinda sore about that,” he admitted.

“I don’t blame you.”

“Thanks,” he said, letting it go like dandelion seeds on a breeze. We pulled up to the motel. Or as close to it that we could get. There was shit everywhere. Flotsam and jetsam littering the sidewalk, broken glass, wood, plastic, car parts, a bit of everything. I saw a soup can roll by. We opened the door and went inside.

“Angela, be careful someone could still be in here . . .” the coyote said, looking around at the disheveled room, assuming some person had done this as part of the chaotic condition of the neighborhood.

“Oh, no don’t worry, this is from the creature, from before,” I calmly explained.

“So what happens now?” The coyote asked, obviously uncomfortable with not knowing much about what was happening but trying his hardest to mask it. Coyote’s hate not knowing what is going on.

So what happens now? Where are we going to ? The echo of the song played again in my memory. It was so annoying. Could you ever really get a song out of your head once you listened to it? Memory was a real mother fucker.

“We have to remove your parasite,” I said, like I had any clue at all how to do that.

“Right, um, no offense or anything Angela, but what does that mean?” The coyote asked with a worried look splashing across his face, he could tell I was less than confident about it too.

“Well, this is the hard part . . . I’m not sure, I have never taken one out before and you could die. Mine was taken out by the creature. That’s the only reason I know that you have one and that it needs to be removed. I can see it right now,” I explained, cringing.

"Can't we just leave it there and do whatever it is we need to do? I'm fine, it's gross to think about having a tapeworm thing on me, but it's fine. I don't want to die Angela, no thanks." Coyotes only fight one thing, death. I was glad he said that and I was filled with a feeling of relief that he would not die, simply because he didn't want to. He had a strong will to live, ha, Willy I laughed.

"I don't think that will work. I totally get it though, you want to keep it on you because you are afraid of dying and I have to say that's a good thing, I mean, what kind of choice is that? Of course you are gonna choose to keep it, that's why we still have these fuckers tagging along. But here is the thing, the creature is killing you, only really slowly, so although it is true that you might die if I take it off, you *will* die if I don't, does that make sense? I feel weird. I have never had to say that to someone before I feel like, like I'm a doctor or something," I mused.

"Oh, sure kid, doctor Angela," the coyote griped, but he digested what I had said. His eyes dropped to the floor as he thought about it.

"Ok, ok so basically I have to give you an . . . exorcism?" My voice rose unnaturally high at the end making it seem like I was asking him rather than telling him.

"Wow, you sound so certain. What, you mean, like the movie, with crucifixes and stuff? Do we need to get a priest?" He chortled.

"I'm not really super sure, I think it's probably not going to be anything we think it is, if there is one thing I am learning it is that things aren't the thing that I think they are," I answered infallibly.

"Well how do you do it? Do you know what to do? How do you know what you are supposed to do? You can't just fake it till you make it with an exorcism, this isn't karaoke," he asked, nearly squealing from disbelief.

"No, no it's ok don't worry I have a book," I answered reassuringly.

"Oh a book, I feel so safe now, a book that changes everything," he sneered. I started digging around in the room, shuffling around some things on the floor and pulled out the bible.

"Oh no . . ." The coyote stared in disbelief. "You gotta be kidding me."

"I know how this looks and I'm sorry. There is no way you can help me unless we get that thing off you, you don't understand, you are way too dampened to be able to even properly move around, much less go up against Asher. You will die then for sure."

"Dampened? What do you mean?" The coyote asked, I kept having flashbacks of my questions to Asher haunt me in ghostly eulogies.

"You can't face Asher unless you get this thing off of you because as soon as you stand in front of him or even get closer to him your parasite is going to see Asher and it's going to leave and you are totally gonna fall to the floor and have a spaz attack and flop around like a fish and he is going to just win or whatever," I said, out of breath from the force of trying to explain something pretty unexplainable. He just stood there swaying from one foot to the other, quietly thinking. I was getting impatient. I purposefully fucked with him by putting my hand up to the disgusting greasy oily black manta mass of goo and almost poking it in its beady little eye. It winced sharply as it withdrew from me and the coyote lurched forward and threw up on the floor. He looked up at me, trembling.

"Ok, you made your point. Let's do it, let's just get it over with. If it makes this gargantuan tarantula take off, it will be worth risking death so I never have to feel it inside of me again!" he said, trying to make light of his fear. "Just tell me what you need me to do." His shoulders slumped forward. I had the feeling that this man, this poor coyote had never uttered those words to anyone in his life. He was always in charge and no one told him what to do, this was new for him, uncomfortable. Here he was, so sad, like looking at a butterfly with its wings plucked off. No coyote should have to suffer this kind of taming, it made me depressed to see his wild spirit wilting, but it was necessary, he would become his true self once he wriggled out of that damn parasitic muck.

"Ok, you better lie down on the floor, because you are going to fall down anyway, so this will save you from a head injury," I instructed.

"Good lookin out," he said, clearing out a spot for himself, away from his own vomit.

"Here, take this to squeeze when it gets really bad," I said, handing him a pillow. He looked up at me, a scared little kid. I opened the middle of the bible and frantically flipped the pages till I found the right one, the psalm, what was it, where was it? Aha. found it, bingo. I raised my head and tried to muster up as much authority as I could;

"His love endureth forever!" I shouted with as much Shakespearean attitude as I could muster, placing the palm of my hand on his forehead, trying to mimic what Asher had done. I felt like a thespian though, I didn't really feel it. Nothing happened. The coyote looked at me and just pretended everything was ok and kept squeezing the pillow, waiting patiently.

Should have worked, I thought to myself. Asher just touched me with his finger on my forehead and the thing hightailed it. I figured since I could see it and Asher could see it, that should be enough. But it had to be something inside him, something Asher had that I didn't, or something I couldn't understand yet. I started to get angry thinking that Asher was more powerful than me and I felt my emotions churning. I had to focus, I had to think. Oh God, if the fate of the world depended on me figuring something out, we were in trouble. I tried to relax and just looked at the coyote. I got really quiet for a moment and just watched the parasite, looked deeply into it. It had to be about my presence, I didn't need a bible, it had to be something I could do. Asher wasn't special, I could do this too, I could do it, I thought, filling myself with arrogance.

"Forget this, " I said, dropping the bible down into the dense polyester layer covering the cement floor. "I don't need to mimic anyone." The coyote's eyes were pressed tightly closed and he pried one of them open to a slit to see what I was going to do while he held onto the pillow with all his might. I reached my hand around to the back of his head where my fingers met a cool slimy lichen feeling from the entity. It was trying to wriggle away from me like jello when it felt my intention. The coyote's head turned traumatically, each vertebrae cracking, a Jacob's ladder against each other. So noisy. I stared at it closer, and closer, I tried not to blink. Then I did it, I caught its gaze. It was like staring into some rave trance video for electronic music. All I saw was repeating geometric patterns, trying to throw me off, but I kept going and piercing into its soul. Don't blink, I told myself.

"Now I gotcha," I said in a deep, assured whisper. I had it. My mind dived inside of it, I don't know how but I just did, without breaking my gaze, I entered the abominable thing. My hand went through its body as though it was not even there as my consciousness grasped it as tight as a fist. The coyote convulsed and moaned. I had penetrated him with my hand, as though he were a misty fog. I didn't breathe, didn't move and drove my fingers into the writhing thing, as deep as I could go, consuming it with my awareness, trying to replace it with myself like a virus. Haha what better way to kill a parasite than with a mind virus? Seemed appropriate. I filled it with my mind through my fingers.

My sentience entered into the thing and it was horrible. I was experiencing everything about this creature, it was so gross, I wanted to throw up. There was a taste in my mouth, chemical and foreign, like I had licked poisonous metal. I could see so much information and memory from it, from coyote, things I didn't want to see but couldn't shut out as the stream screamed into me. The thing had been there with him, the coyote, since his birth. I saw the parasite being a peeping Tom, watching the coyote's spirit enter into his mother, he just dropped right down into her like he was falling into a hole or going down a slide, the creature slung a tentacle like a lasso and joined the ride. I could sense where the parasite had come from, it was like . . . in another place, another location. I felt deeper into it with my fingers and saw something I wasn't expecting, stars. It was beautiful. There were interstellar trails, like nebulae and unfamiliar shapes with strange shapes. It seemed that though these entities had attached to us, for quite a while, they hadn't always been here, they came from somewhere else in outer space. When the creature felt me coming into this knowledge it knew my judgments and answered me somehow, it showed me that I also was not from here. There was a seed of me that had been propelled, like a rocket through star trails, there was a bird of some sort I was riding on, before I had been Angela. The parasite was trying to tell me that we were also parasites, humans were no better than it was. The thing was trying to defend its honor at my attempt to look down upon it for being a hitchhiker.

"You are like me," it thought into me disdainfully. I blushed, embarrassed to realize I had no idea where humans came from, we had all forgotten that morsel of our background long ago. I didn't even know my great great grandparents. It looked into me, into Jake and I shuddered at the realization that Jake did not have a parasite. It was studying Jake's body as though it were alien, making me wonder if Jake ever had a parasite? Why was it thinking it was so strange that Jake didn't have a hitchhiker? Could it see me inside of Jake? The parasite could read my thoughts just as I could see into it and it answered me;

"He's dead, you fool." It was talking about Jake. Jake was dead. I didn't get it. What the fuck was it talking about? Jake was a dream person, I wasn't sure he had ever even been alive. I started to lose it and I knew it was time to disengage, I had to unravel my mind from this thing. Who knows what was really true, and I would be Goddamned if I was going to trust the mind of a parasite, I had to just keep doing the job I was there to do. Remove the fucking thing. I turned my concentration to the task and shifted my intention, it felt me and started to squirm.

"1, 2, 3," I counted out loud, and the coyote braced himself, compressing the pillow in a vice of arms and legs. As quickly as I could, I yanked it out of him with all my strength and stood up to shoot it like a rocket into the ceiling. I was a barbarian raising my sword up to catch a shimmer of the setting Sun. I lifted my hand all the way up, grasping the pulsing blob, still locked into its tiny red eyes. The strange life form faded, becoming transparent within seconds of leaving his body.

I looked down to see if he was ok, he was motionless but in such a way it seemed impossible, he was suspended in time. I remembered now, myself when the thing was leaving me, my body revolted at the memory and resisted, it did not want to return to that place and I tried to force my mind off where it was seeking to go. I took a deep breath in and relaxed my grip on the thing as it floated away to God only knows where, through the window and I sat down on the floor next to the coyote. The bottom dweller stopped for a moment gazing back at Willy and I could feel it saying something to him, a farewell, just as mine had. The coyote shot out of the suspension and crumpled on the floor. I touched his side, worried. He was still breathing. I did it. I fucking did it. I felt just as powerful as Asher in that moment and started to feel like I could take on an interdimensional entity. I slumped down and rested there on the floor with him, in the middle of a huge pile of trash, on the cringy carpet, we were both sweating profusely. His breathing quickened and he rustled around a bit, coming to.

"Good morning," I said in an annoyingly cheerful tone.

"Looks like we did it kid," he said, proud of himself, and of me. He sharply winced at the sound of his own voice and I remembered he was coming into the intense hyper perceptivity of reality.

"Don't worry," I whispered, "It will chill out, the parasites make you a bit dull around the edges. Everything is going to be pretty amplified for a while, but you'll get used to it."

"What do we do now?" he asked, laughing at the ridiculousness of the question, lowering his voice and getting visibly distracted by the surroundings he was only just now seeing as they truly were. I saw his eyes focusing on the window, on the walls, on his hands. He was starting to stare too closely at his hands. Been there, done that. So much to explain to him, I had to just keep moving. I had total understanding for Asher at that moment. There was a vast sea we couldn't see, so much people would never understand unless they went through unfathomable transformations. The job of getting everyone up to speed seemed impossible as here, with just one person, I was unable to get through to them everything that I had come to understand. The transference of knowledge seemed like an impossible task to me at that moment. I couldn't explain things to him and had to hope he could let go of the need to control things enough to be receptive.

"Don't be scared, I know just what to do," I answered him confidently. "We have to go to sleep," I concluded.

"What?" he said, raising an eyebrow, squinting because he had spoken too loudly. "How the fuck am I going to go to sleep? I feel like I just smoked crack!" he seethed, grinding his teeth and feeling his own tongue in his mouth as if for the first time. He looked like an infant playing with their mouth and toes as though they were disconnected objects. He kept twitching around like a tweaker, had I looked like that to Asher I wondered, suddenly embarrassed.

"I know, I know it's crazy, and I wish we had more time. We have to get back into the underworld while I can still sleep, honestly I'm not sure how much longer I have to be able to still fall asleep. We need to move quickly and figure it out as we go. All I know is that I need you there with me," I said, a bit sheepishly.

"You mean I'm going to stop sleeping?" he said, clearly disturbed and focusing on the wrong bit of information I just relayed.

"Yes, if everything works," I said, wondering aloud to myself.

"What? What happens if everything doesn't work?" he retorted.

"Um I really don't have the slightest idea! Isn't it wonderful?! It's completely new and has never happened before! I don't think anyone knows what's going to happen next! Isn't it the best thing ever? Each moment we are having now is totally not like anything else! It's so incredible!" I said, grinning maniacally.

"Man, there is no double fucking way I am going to fall asleep, just no way. No way, no how. You are going to have to come up with something else," he said, his leg shaking nervously in a rhythm only he could hear. I knew I was going to have to force him, I couldn't sit around explaining things he wouldn't understand anyway, I had no idea what Asher was up to while we were here fighting about sleeping.

I made a resolve with my mind to make him sleep and he sensed it as I settled into my feet. He recoiled and fear rose up in him. He didn't know what to expect from me anymore, and neither did I. I put my hand on his forehead. I didn't want to dominate him, I just had to in order to save time.

Sleep. My mind shouted into him. I knew it would work because I had commanded myself the same thing. I guess it was a kind of aggressive hypnosis. The kickboxing of hypnotism. Convincing myself to listen to myself was much harder than forcing myself onto others, which was interesting. Since I had accomplished it already, now it was easy, like riding a bicycle. He crumpled onto the floor into the pile of trash, passed out. Oops, I guess it's not very nice to control him that way but I didn't have much choice, we had to act fast. At least I didn't fucking cut open his arm, unlike some people. I took my same hand and placed it over my own head and repeated the command, like a far away adventurer shouting "open sesame." I sank to the bottom of the ocean as the tide rose over me. I heard sounds now. I had done this enough times I could finally feel it, discern it, it really was a kind of falling. No wonder they called it falling asleep, it was a descent. Not really water, but it was waves, the waves were rings of sound hitting my body. I could discern each level like going in an elevator that had different notes, descending through a rainbow of musical scales. My mind couldn't shake the feeling that the parasite had been right, and that I was occupying the body of a dead man. Was I a zombie? Was death a kind of sleep where we dream forever? I imagined all the people with the yellow eyes and hairy bodies were all dead people and I became very unsettled as I slipped into the land of the lost.

THE HUNT

Slowly seeping in, the sounds invaded my auditory canal. A low grumbling growl was growing. He was shaking me awake, he was scared. Poor coyote, this must be quite a shock. At least I had the advantage of knowing everything was insane because a naked man fell through the roof, expanding my idea of the impossible. I opened my eyes and I could see why the coyote was so concerned. There was nothing there, nothing but the red grid. Everything had gone, the underworld was empty. The expanse seemed to stretch on for quite some time, maybe even an infinity. It was hard to tell which way was up, the sky looked the same as the ground, we were in some amorphous energetic field.

Well that's upsetting. I wasn't talking though, only thinking, he could hear me, I could hear his thoughts too. I felt a tickle in my belly as my thought traveled into his awareness, his lucidity. It was natural now, we could sense each other. A layer had been lifted away and we could fluidly traverse the space between us with our thoughts. There was no barrier or hiding things within the safe caverns of our skulls. The sensation was coming from my belly, not my brain like I would have thought. When we spoke this way to each other, I wasn't feeling the thoughts in my head as I usually did, I could feel them right in the middle of my gut. It was the same as what Asher had stirred up in me during our fight, deep inside me, the same location.

I saw what the parasite showed you too you know. The coyote thought. *I think it's right, I think you are in some dead guy's body.*

Why do you think that? I pondered into him.

Something about your eyes, I mean his eyes, I mean the eyes you are looking out of, they look weird, like empty. I know you are in there, but they just look vacant, I don't know how to describe it. Is it this place . . . are we in the land of the dead? The coyote asked me, I could tell he was creeped out.

I don't know man, I don't get it, how can the place you go when you dream be the same place you go when you die? How can that be? Is everyone who is dreaming just hanging out with dead people? What is it? I was asking both myself and him.

I don't know, kid, but this place doesn't make much sense no matter how you look at it. The coyote thought, looking around at the emptiness and the confusing geometry surrounding us. *How are we supposed to find Asher? This place is a nightmare.* Coyote thought into me.

I need to find a book. I replied assuredly. We looked around.

Yea, that might be a problem. He thought back, looking around. *Wait a minute, I don't have a book, but maybe this will help . . .*

What? I asked.

I do have my pocket notebook, and it's weird because it's grid paper, like this place, ha. I got it because it seemed more professional when I pulled it out in front of people, it made me feel like an architect. He reached into his pants and pulled out a little red notebook that was a few inches across with wire spiral bound loops across the top and a pen stuck through them. Something fell to his feet as he was extracting the notebook from his pants and he looked down. An expression of utter delight coated his face as he bent, cracking his knees to pick up a pack of cigarettes he had apparently forgotten about and pulled one out placing it promptly in his mouth. He dug his hand swiftly into his front pocket to produce his lighter. He had erased all thoughts about me and our task in that brief interlude between seeing the nicotine and became obsessively focused on lighting up. I just patiently sat there and watched him, fascinated by his ritual pleasure, kind of jealous that he had something like that to instantly take his mind off things. I hated smoking though, always had, it was so painful for me, I just didn't get it, my body revolted when I tried and I had only a repulsion for the habit. He inhaled deeply and ecstatically as the flame hit the tobacco and his eyes rolled back in his face. After taking a few puffs he looked at me, snapping back into the situation.

Can I see it? I motioned to the notebook that was still in his grip. Who knows what might work in this place. I snatched it from his hand and stared at it as he stood there incredibly happy that he could still smoke in the underworld. I held the pad for a moment and carefully tried to find the middle with my fingers. I flung it open to its estimated center, curious to see what might happen. All I saw was a bunch of phone numbers. I whisked my eyes to him and he had a crooked grin, obscured by smoke wafting through his lips. They were women's phone numbers. I tried not to be judgy and just kept flipping through the paper, ignoring some childish pornographic sketches. I came to a few blank pages and took the pen out of the wire. As I did so, a memory possessed my mind. Time shifted and I found myself in elementary school, looking down at a piece of graph paper.

Hey, remember back in school, I began to include him in my nostalgia and he interrupted me dramatically.

School is for suckers. He responded without skipping a beat, blowing out a cloud of smoke.

Ok anyway, when I was in school we would do these dumb math problems and I never really understood the point and you had to like, draw these lines and make them on graph paper and you had to create an axis and then plot things in it and make shapes. They use them to make all those charts and graphs for business people.

Oh yea, of course I've seen those, I'm not stupid. What about it? He defended his lack of education.

We are really in one of those right now. A grid is like that, a place to plot points in space, to create, to create . . . I wrestled to find the words with my thoughts.

Create what? He asked, trying to solve the equation.

A location, to create a location. I thought at last. *When you make a cross with lines, you create a location.*

What does that mean? A location is just there, it just is a place that's there you can't create it with dots. He seemed sensible, even though we were in the underworld standing on a giant grid, yes that makes sense. One thing I was learning was how difficult it was for humans to abandon their minds to the reality of the irrational.

Exactly! Where is it? Haha this is so hilarious. We think the location is a place because we can't see behind it, or . . . under it. The place the location is, is on a grid like this, that's where the place is. Maybe it's, like, born there? There is usually stuff, in the overworld so you don't notice it, but underneath it all looks like this, kind of like your bones underneath your skin. I gleefully exclaimed, knowing I was somehow right even though I had no idea what I was talking about.

Huh? You lost me. He admitted.

Think about a map, like coordinates, yes coordinates. Like Longitude and latitude. I know it looks like we are nowhere because there is nothing here, but that's not true. I thought, feeling the sentience growing in me, a geyser about to spout. *We aren't nowhere! We are everywhere! We are anywhere! It's just folded into itself so we can't see it! We have to plot it out!* If there was a way you could think-shout I just did it.

Ooookay? He was still confused. I had to stop trying to explain it to him, it was useless, I just had to do it. An idea slapped me in the face. I could make a map of all the places, of everything I could remember since Asher emerged. A memory map, charting thoughts for a brainstorm. The places I had been to in the dreams, there was something I could do, to put them in an image, locate them on a map, picture them all together. I had to get organized.

I ripped out the blank pages and lined them up so I had more space, making a bigger square out of the smaller rectangles. Weird you can make a square out of rectangles I thought. The pieces of paper looked like when I played the game "memory" with cards and they were all turned over and you had to remember where the matches were. I giggled to myself while the coyote just watched me confoundedly. I furiously plotted points on the paper like a psycho putting pins in things, connecting them with yarn on a bulletin board to create a conspiracy theory. I backed away and took in everything I had scribbled down on the paper. From a distance that form of everything I had put together inside of the square was a circle. How had that even happened? How could I have randomly drawn out all that only to make a perfect circle, fit snugly within the square. It was a globe, a map of a world. A sphere had formed, just like the Earth, I told myself. Huh, I wondered if every map would make a circle no matter what you did. This map must be a ring because the shape of the realm is a sphere, just like the Earth. How does that work? I wondered, if the Earth is a sphere, well unless you argue with folk on the internet about it being flat, if the Earth is a sphere and the dream locations make a sphere, are there two different spheres, side by side? Is it a shadow sphere? Are they overlapping, is one inside the other? Whatever, I probably wasn't going to be able to figure it out, how silly is my brain. I just had to sit and observe it. Ugh, I remembered that was the advice Asher had told me, to stop asking questions and just look at things.

I had a circular map of the locations, that meant they should all lead back to the other ones, maybe they circle back to each other, I could retrace my steps and that might make some sort of path or something. Oh no. A clarity crept into me in a slow crawl. There was nothing but the circle, no matter which way I went I would always return, would always circle back, infinitely. I laughed in a twisted cackle. Oh, we think we are so clever, so smart. We are buffoons walking in circles, thinking we are moving when we stand in front of a cycling zoetrope while our feet march in place. Only the background is moving around us, only the background is moving around us. I pondered that for a moment. We are not moving. We are trapped somewhere. There was no other choice, but to go in a circle, it was an ecliptic prison. A prison. I was quickly coming into a lucid realization that everything was a trick, the world was a trick.

What is this place? I asked a different question than I had ever asked before, a new thing. Surely there was another form, some other shape. It can't be only circles, a square? A triangle? Oh no, as I pictured those geometries I understood they all went around as well. Every shape was a closed rotation that came back to meet themselves. Squares, triangles were also circles, because they just revolved back to the place where they started. Would I always just come back to meet myself in the same way as every shape? Was there no escape? Am I a circle? The coyote was watching me with a concerned look on his face. I could tell he was following me but he didn't seem to understand where this was going. I tried to ignore his presence and keep following the thread.

Beginning middle and end, beginning middle and end, my memory was shouting the words to me over and over again. They kept cycling through my mind. Wait, what is the beginning, middle and end of a circle? How can there be any beginning, middle and end at all? The bible Asher had birthed from, was a book, a rectangle, not a circle at all, but I made a heart out of it which also connected back upon itself. Well, I mean how do you draw a circle, how do you start it? My memory went back through its rabbit holes to elementary school again when we were working with the graph paper. My earliest recollection of making a circle was when I received a wound from a schoolmate. Another painful reminder. The teacher had handed out a compass to everyone in the class and was trying to teach us how to use them. A little boy had been running around the classroom poking people with their compass and they had come over to me and asked me to stick out my hand. I could feel Angela's being in the memory, it was more like watching a movie, detached. I trustingly put my hand out and he promptly stabbed it with his compass. I looked at the top of Jake's hand to see if the scar was still there. It wasn't. Asher's scar was still prominent however. You draw a circle by starting in the center. By making a wasp sting, a pinprick, a penetration. The center is the beginning. Time, the way to get to the middle of time was through the center, be here now, I laughed despite myself. Going around in circles in my thoughts was making me dizzy, the middle was the beginning. The beginning was the middle.

Ok, I thought to myself, let's just accept that, the beginning is the middle. That means whatever is in the middle of the map was the way to the beginning and the place everything returns to eventually. Asher had said, I am the beginning and the end. The middle was left out on purpose, the answer was the middle, the center. Hmm. I looked at the map to see what was in the center of it.

There, right smack dab in the middle of the map was the room, the hotel room, terrible daynight elephants and all. It wasn't the room though, it was Asher. Asher was a location. How could a living thing that moved around be a location? I wondered, and in the same instant my mind answered the question; the Earth is a living thing that moves around and is a location. A brief flash of understanding at the edge of a cliff entered me, the Earth for a moment, was a circle but not a circle, it was . . . also something else I couldn't quite understand. I felt the distant song, the spider web, the thing dreaming us again. The reason the hotel room was at the center was because that was where Asher first came through, was born, I had to keep my mind straight. That was the answer, I had to find Asher, and the way I would do that was to get the book, the location was the form of Asher from the book.

Everything else had been a shadow, a cheap imitation in the underworld, searching for the book in the places was just trying to recreate that moment in another location, recreate Asher in another location, like an actor playing someone real on TV. It was a way to bring that moment into another place by making a mimic of it, by copying it, reproducing it somehow, and that was only possible because it had already been done. Like looking at a picture of someone who had lived a long time ago. Could anything already done be replicated in this way I wondered? Was everything just a cheap knock off of some original that had been made, God only knows how long ago? I must have even somehow replicated an action which brought Asher through to begin with. I was only repeating something someone had planned and done before by bringing Asher through, this cannot have been the first time, this wasn't new. This was a ring, a circus.

Everything that existed was a ripple extending from some center somewhere. A jerk spasmed within me, that familiar twinge of discomfort I was ensconced in when Asher was talking about me being enfolded in myself. I was pregnant with some mystery thing within me. I could use my memory to plot the location and go there. I could recapture, with enough cognizance and return, by walking in a circle. I could also be a location, I realized. After all, I'm here, in time, in space, moving, albeit in circles I am the Sun, the center of the revolving space around me and I could do it too. I could do it too. Just like the Earth. I am an Earth trapped in an ecliptic prison. I walked in a circle while remembering the moment of Asher's appearance, I looked at coyote

Follow me. He didn't bat an eye and fell in step. We traced the outline of a circle on the grid by cutting diagonally through the cubes. He hadn't even resisted when I told him what to do, just believed me. Although I knew I had come to understand things, something about having someone else there to back you up did feel really good, like a boost. Suddenly, it was there, it just appeared like magic in the center of the circle we had been walking. The book. It was the Goddamn bible. I'd recognize that shitty pleather cover anywhere. The coyote stopped walking and stared in disbelief. Our steps themselves had opened a space for it to come through.

Now we can go to Asher. We have to somehow put him back in the book. That's all I know, I thought-spoke to him in the utmost of certainty.

How do we do that? he asked eager to end whatever had begun. I opened the book, and somehow, my fingers landed on the center Psalm.

The Green Bitch

We landed clumsily, face to face with no space in between, staring into Asher's eyes. Asher jerked back, we had surprised it. I smiled, we had the upper hand. An unexpected thing seemed shocking for one that claimed to be able to see everything. Feasibly, this was not the case in the underworld, maybe Asher couldn't see everything here, maybe something had changed. We still had time, we had a chance. Asher leapt away from us and I looked right into its eyes. I saw the countenance up close for the first time, saw my appearance, my old face and it stopped me in my tracks. Angela was so beautiful. I had never thought of myself as beautiful before. I couldn't stop staring. A deluge of memories overtook all other thoughts as I was filled again with Angela. I had to keep her out, at least right now. That wasn't me, I mean I wasn't her right now. What a mind fuck.

"**How?**" Asher's voice invaded our minds with an aggressive intensity, staring at the coyote's lack of his parasitic companion. I guess Asher hadn't expected that I would be successful in clearing the parasite off anyone else, perhaps they thought only they could do it. He couldn't understand how the coyote was here with us. Maybe Asher had never had a friend, I distantly ruminated. Asher looked at coyote now and spoke into his mind, I could hear them both, though Asher tried to shut me out;

"Fool, do not be tricked by her. She seeks to use you. Think, my friend, on how she has already made use of you to be thrown away. She cares not for your life, for who you are. You are here as her servant to do her bidding which is nothing but a petty attack upon me. You follow her like a dog. Leave her now and come with me, join me, she is only trying to imitate me, she seeks the power for herself. She will never give you power." Asher was influencing him because it was coming from Angela's lips, I could see the pull. It was messing with the coyote's mind and Asher knew it. I wasn't mad at the coyote, he liked me, what can I say.

Why should I trust you? Coyote thought back to Asher. *It was you who took her from me, how do I know she would have left if you hadn't told her to?* Coyote thought into them.

"I am trying to do something bigger, something great. You can perish with her now or join me to vindicate yourself in all eternity. It's your choice." Asher stopped and looked at me, into my eyes, he saw what happened, he saw everything. He started talking again. "I can see you have somehow both figured out this is the place of the dying ones and you seem surprised by this. You are surprised that the body of Jake is dead. As if this body of yours I am in is any different. You live in a graveyard in the overworld, but you can't see it because you are too deadened in your own minds. Everything you use are remnants of the dead, you listen to songs of voices of the dead, live in buildings built by the dead, drive on roads paved by the dead, your parents parents are dead. Soon you both will no longer be in the overworld, but shall fall asleep forever and fall into the Earth and be here, yet you have no interest in helping me solve this. How do I deal with that level of ignorance, how do I tell you that you are already dead because you wont wake up? All of you are forever dead!" Asher shouted. "You don't understand and even when you are here, dead forever, with all the other corpses, you won't know because you will be asleep and you will forget everything!" Asher's eyes widened with fury. I couldn't really handle what Asher was saying but I had to just think about it as more lies, I couldn't trust anything they said. There was no way I could know if anything was true anymore, I had to just keep going. All I knew was that I couldn't trust them.

Shhh shhh shhh, don't listen. I tried to think to the coyote privately to keep Asher veiled. I focused on trying to remember smelling cigarettes to direct it to him. He was fixedly concentrated on Asher because they looked like Angela. I could tell he couldn't shake her off. I watched his mind wondering if that was really Angela and if I had been lying, trying to trick him.

I am glad we are friends, Willy. You have stuck by me, I see you, I value you. I trust you, I promise. I said the last reluctantly but with full surrender because I knew it was true even though I didn't want it to be. Asher could feel the truth of it too and raised her hands up into the air, she looked like she was preparing something. I didn't want to find out what it was. Her eyes were closed. I had to act fast. I opened the bible still in my grasp at random and commanded it

"Speak!" I shouted out loud. I dropped my gaze and read the line in a shrill shriek.

"When two or more are gathered in my name, there I am. I am with them." I didn't even think, I just acted spontaneously as though I was being guided by an unseen force, light was starting to come out of Asher's palms now, I only had a few seconds.

Quick hold this, I shoved the bible, split down the center to the coyote and put my hand on it

"Double!" I yelled at the book. Another bible appeared in my hand, a duplicate! We both smiled, amazed that it worked! Filled with wonder, I looked at the page number and opened the clone to the same page and dropped them right on top of each other so that the identical pages touched each other in a kiss, making a mirror. I couldn't help but laugh as my mind had the thought that it was just like me facing my own face, Angela's face through different eyes, a thing confronted with itself, a reflection.

Look at me, look into my eyes. I told the coyote and we locked our gaze. I felt him wince at Jake's face after seeing Angela again.

Focus on me. our eyes were doubled, in a pair of pairs. Could it be, that due to a simple thing, such a simple thing as a friend, another person to gather with, that we would be victorious? Just then, we looked over and lightning was starting to precipitate in the air around Asher's hands.

Oh no, the coyote thought. Then, quiet as a whisper something happened.

I am here. A new voice, low and sultry invaded everything. As I heard this new voice, another being appeared at our side, in between me and the coyote. We were now three pairs of eyes. She was there, she was completely green. The energy around her was pulsing and cycling as if trapped within a never ending orgasm. It was hard to tell what shape she was, she kept moving. The color green filled our view. My eyes had a hue to them now, as did the coyote's, I could see it in the green light as though we were at a rave under a black light. I hadn't seen it before, strange I thought, my eyes could see everything but themselves. It was like it was coming from behind them. The coyote's eyes were orange, and mine were violet. I saw Asher's eyes, for the first time, they were red. Flaming red like a burning tiger. I peered deeply into them, I saw a burning tiger wrapped around a panther in the center that felt like it was going to leap out at me. I was haunted by a place I had been before and saw myself evaporating, coyote noticed it too and was distraught. I had to break the link, I dug my thumb into my arm to stay here, and looked over at the new being that had burst forth. Her eyes were glowing green in an emerald fire.

We had unfolded another entity, and her presence was warping everything. It was only because we had come together, the coyote and I, I could not have done this by myself. We didn't really even like each other, but yet here we were, come together because we had to. That was what brought her in. One for the first, two for the second.

"No! This cannot be!" Asher shouted, it was fully enraged now, and thrusted his lightning bolt fingers at all of us. We all tried not to blink, the green woman's effect had created a shield that surrounded us.

Do not be afraid. Her voice was calm and soothing inside our heads. Asher was trying to break through the shield, he was going after her now, he forgot all about us. Asher's sparking hands were going straight for her neck and the face of Angela had transformed into something hard to describe, it was horrific. The eyes had sunken into the skull and were seething scarlet, almost like the parasite's eyes, but they were slightly different, there was something . . . older about them, something ancient. I couldn't believe I hadn't noticed it before. The green woman was forcing it out, revealing it, just with her presence, dropping the mask. Asher had his fingers buried into her throat now, but she was still standing there, calmly smiling, her feet were growing roots into the ground, if there even was a ground in this place, and she wasn't budging as the voltages were visibly catching her flesh on fire, everything was red and green like Christmas. We all just kept staring, looking directly into the smoldering crimson eyes. Coyote and I had to take a few steps back due to the severity of the electricity. My mouth tasted like metal. A writhing rift in her abdomen swelled. There was a glowing ball in her midsection where her umbilicus would have been, if she even had one, and it was expanding very rapidly. The shine intensified and Asher's face dropped. The hands were stuck, lodged in her neck now and Asher was frantically flailing, trying to escape. Asher moved his feet up to try and push itself off of her body, only to find they became embedded, Asher was an appendage on her, becoming absorbed into her skin everywhere they were contacting each other. Her smile lunged wider and wider, like a clown in a bad movie, her teeth elongated into fangs. She just kept smiling back at Asher who was a rat caught in a glue trap, pitiful and terrified. She had welcomed the attack because she knew it would only link Asher closer to her.

Asher withdrew their gaze, breaking eye contact with her and looking right into me instead. I saw a shriveled set of shrugged shoulders containing a thin frame of withered wisps where Asher once was. The bowed head begrudgingly rose up to meet my puzzled gaze, and the eyes I beheld grabbed me by my very veins and shook the blood to its deepest recesses. When I looked into Asher's eyes the whole history of the world came flapping into my mind like an army of bats filling every cavernous corner, making all else dark with their wings.

As soon as Asher's line of sight withdrew, The green woman's mouth opened and the luminous sphere from her gut rose up through her body, into her throat, lodging itself in her sharp teeth. She closed her eyes slowly, smirking a supernatural grin and a pulse of lightning emerged, so strong all the hairs on my body stood up on end. She surged at Asher, striking them, enveloping and scorching them in a green flame. She had no power and only had returned what Asher had poured into her, tit for tat in childish reciprocity that was terrifyingly effective. Instant karma was a bitch.

I watched Asher collapse and crumple up on the ground as their hands and feet were singed out of the green woman, turning into piles of ash and dust. I saw myself in Asher in that moment, it could have been because Asher had taken my body, which was now totally destroyed, or it could have been because I had finally found my empathy, or maybe some kind of combination of the two. The result of Asher's annihilation was that I could finally view from their perspective instead of just my own. When my feeling of threat had passed, the dark cloud that had been obscuring my vision moved out of the way. It was a terrible feeling, regret and shame poured into me like wet cement. My stomach hurled and I wanted to die. This wasn't what I desired, but I had caused this. I killed Asher. The weight of this responsibility bored into me like a tick and I fell to my knees. Whoever said revenge was sweet must have been a psychopath. Vengeance was as bad as the violation, what misery. The suffering was all consuming, moving me past any personal feelings of betrayal, all I could see was Asher's despair, all I felt was grief.

I looked down at the body there, pitifully folded in upon itself. Enfolded, I thought to myself. Back into the book I guess. I stared at the remains, which were also my remains, my corpse, the form Angela had been. An impotent ennui for Asher pooled where once my obsessive outrage had been. Even though he had tried to ruin everything, all I had known was wrong. Was it so bad for Asher to destroy what the world had been? Why should he suffer? I wept. I didn't care what he had done. I could only see the sad decay, the horrible result of the victory, there was no satisfaction in it. I knew him, I had spoken to him, he helped me. Why? Why was this happening? I ran over to him, the coyote tried to grab my arm but it was too late, I was too fast. I knelt beside him, full of guilt and shame for what had happened. Full of lament for the suffering of everything.

I opened the bible and picked up a handful of the ashes that were left of Asher and sprinkled it onto the pages of the center, at the psalm, hoping someday, like a phoenix the remains could resurrect themselves when they would be able to try again, get another chance, maybe find someone who wasn't as stupid as me. Maybe everything could be recapitulated from its ashes. I raised my gaze up to the sunless sky and I spoke on his behalf. I wasn't one for prayer, I mostly just complained and questioned, but a sincere wish rose up in my throat.

Please, whatever is there, why does Asher need to come to an end just because he wanted to help? It could be true that he went too far, but I want you to know that I don't blame him, I hope that you don't either, please have mercy on him, have mercy. My mind was contorting trying to make sense of everything that had happened, to see past myself to the truth. I collapsed and wept in my useless realizations over the lifeless mannequin. He had been right, I had not known what love was. I didn't understand. I don't understand anything.

My laments were interrupted as I saw the green woman out of the corner of my eye, she was approaching me. I looked up at her hoping for some kind of wisdom or consolation to be imparted from this divine being. She knelt down quietly and reached out, placing her hands on what was left of Asher's body. I quickly felt a wave of nausea overtake me out of nowhere, it didn't feel right. It was so odd that you could feel things so physically here in the dream world I mused as my entrails convulsed. I could only stare in despair as the green woman's shape changed. I swiveled my eyeballs over at the coyote who had broken out in a clammy sweat, he too was staring, motionless, terrified. Her lips were moving and smacking, cracking unnaturally until her entire lower jaw unhinged itself as she gagged and gurgled from within her throat. I couldn't breathe or move, the coyote and I seemed to be paralyzed by whatever was about to transpire which we had no control of whatsoever. She bent down with her gaping maw and wrapped it around the ankle stubs left on Asher's corpse. Overtaken by revulsion, breaking out in goosebumps on my skin, she was going to eat Asher, and not just eat them, but swallow them whole.

She dropped her arms to her side and lay down flat on the ground on her belly and worked her way slowly up the body. We couldn't move, couldn't do anything, I tried to scream but nothing came out. She made us watch, she was making us watch her. I was watching Asher's, Angela's, my body be devoured right in front of me. She was eating them like a fucking boa constrictor. Her mouth wriggled like loose elastic, writhing over the cadaver. Her eyes were wide and empty, vapid of any kind of emotion at all. Even pleasure was nowhere to be seen, it was a drastically perfunctory occasion for her.

We watched the head go down her gullet and we realized that it would soon be over and then another thing would happen. What if it eats us too? I couldn't help but have the thought. I worked with my mind and comprehended that I had to stop thinking anything because I didn't want the green woman to hear my mind. I regretted thinking the thought as soon as it had been let out, afraid I would give her any ideas. Everything on full display, each invasive suggestion up and out for all to see. I tried to focus on feeling my breath and my body. Don't think, I thought to myself. I tried to smell the memory of coyote's cigarettes in his car to the point where I could imagine the smoke entering me so that I could focus and direct;

Don't think. I thought-spoke to him. He didn't answer me and kept very still. We could only sit and watch. She finished her "meal" and stood up, composing herself. Her body bent and wiggled in a very disturbing way, cracking and squishing. She didn't seem to care about us at all. Her mission seemingly accomplished, she looked around and walked away. I had to quell all the questions that were trying so hard to rise up in my mind, it was like reigning in wild horses that threatened to stampede at any moment.

"Steady" I tried to soothe myself. I couldn't help feeling like I had just jumped out of the frying pan into the fire. The thing we did to control the threat of Asher seemed far more menacing and horrible. I had just tried to kill a cockroach with a tidal wave. What a fool I am. What a fool.

The green woman broke off a piece of the red grid as she was walking and shoved it into her face. Lightning was coming off her from what she'd absorbed in the battle with Asher and she just kept shedding electricity and eating everything in her path. We remained still, unmoving until she disappeared from our view.

We looked around, hoping everything would have gone back to normal now that Asher was gone. Wishing everything would magically be reset by what we had done in sacrifice to the greater good. Maybe everyone would just go back to sleep and the dream realm would go back to what it used to be. I looked down at myself and took a long deep sigh. I was still Jake. Coyote gave me a rather disappointed look as well, I don't think he liked Jake much at all, especially seeing the ruined form of his former crush turned into a snack. This made me laugh in Jake's booming, bass filled voice. The coyote cringed his face, he didn't seem to find it as funny as I did.

What do we do now? The coyote thought helplessly.

So what happens now? I sang Evita to myself within my mind, thinking about the fact that the person who had written and sung that song was dead now, just as Asher had pointed out.

I mean is everything just like this now? Coyote continued. *How are we going to live in the world, in the underworld? Everything is going to shut down, we failed. Does that mean everyone is going to die, like Asher said? Are we dead now?* The coyote was starting to lose it.

The underworld has not disappeared though, I reasoned with him. *We are still here, even if we are trapped inside it with that . . . .thing, whatever it was.* It dawned upon me that we were all going to be trapped here in a sleepless night until enough of us woke up. No! I fully envisioned what a terrible thing it was that Asher was gone. He was the bridge. We were trapped now because we had defeated him. I hung my head in agony. No one fucking even knew that they had to wake up now and they certainly weren't going to listen to me. Think Angela, Jake whoever the fuck I am now. Think. What was I supposed to do without Asher? I'll just have to do it myself.

Ahem invaded the coyote's thoughts into me. I forgot, he could hear everything I thought. So uncomfortable.

Oh right haha. I laughed nervously, I looked at him, with true and sincere appreciation. Here he was, still here. He hadn't left which was more than I could say for any other friend I had up until now. What a cosmic joke that the ones who are really there for you are always the ones you don't want around.

If you were really a coyote I guess you would have run away, I teased him.

Hey guess what? he thought, very considerately.

What? I reflected back.

Did you know that coyotes are monogamous and stay with their partners till death? he asked, contorting his face into a grin.

No, I didn't know that, I answered truthfully, smiling.

Well, they do. So I guess you don't know as much about coyotes as you think you do, he said, quite satisfied with himself.

Haha no, I really don't, I thought, playfully bumping his elbow.

Hey! I thought-shouted at him.

Yes, Angela? he replied.

Thank you Willy. I mean it, thanks. You are a true friend. The sincerity filled me in that moment.

You are welcome Angela, Willy replied. In the middle of this place, something as simple as someone who just didn't leave, ended up being my salvation. The power of fidelity had given me a place to abide when the world was unsolid. We could hear each other's thoughts so clearly now, it was like we were riding a roller coaster together, no one needed to say anything. We had a mutual understanding. He thought towards me;

You can do this too Angela. You need to remember your own ability to do things. You can do it. You can bridge them, the upper and under worlds, not just Asher, you can do it too. He was so assured. He believed in me, it was the best gift I had ever received. I nodded at him, holding his gaze.

Now, let's go get my body back from that green bitch, I said.

Right. He nodded.

FULL CIRCLE

The aperture tightened as the liberation of the lucidity flowed into me. My consciousness stood up like a cobra rising after laying prone. I took in my surroundings. I squatted down to feel the ground with my fingertips. I smelled it with my nose. It had a scent, damp and fragrant, just like the Earth, just like the Earth I thought. If you have ever smelled the soil after the rain, it's hard to describe the feeling. So real, I thought to myself I can't tell the difference. I kept testing it, trying to discern what it was that made it different from waking reality. I searched for some kind of structural difference, a hint, a clue that my perceptions could pick up. Memory covered me, the Sun, I thought. I searched everywhere and could not find the Sun. That was it, that was the difference. This was a Sunless land of sleep. I was also different, even what I thought was me, my whole sense of myself. It was me and what I could do that shifted, like water. The environment of the underworld only moved if I moved, otherwise you would never be able to tell you were in the dream realm. It was so real. Haha, so real I laughed to myself, my conclusion on the dream realm was that it was so real. As I thought that thought, so real, I was instantly in a city. The underworld had responded, answering what made it different. I had abilities here I didn't have in the Sun world. I turned over in my mind and it changed my location, it formed a point in time space. I was still in the underworld but I had transport-ed myself. Something about my mind could move me to other places, locations. What was that I thought, a dimension? Is this what people meant when they talked about dimensions?

I looked around to see where my mind had taken me. I was in a li-brary. Coyote wasn't there. Other people were milling about, walking through the stacks of books. Were they even real? Were they all just yellow eyed ape people, I thought, solipsistically. I stood at the foot of a staircase. People were walking up and down the stairs. I watched them. Huh, I thought to myself, when I looked at people in the under-world, they did not have parasites. Hmm, there were no parasites here. I only saw the parasites in the overworld, they couldn't get to people down here for some reason. The underworld was a parasite free place. Perhaps that was part of the reason Asher needed to do the work down here. Something about the underworld did not permit the parasites to enter, but people were asleep, or dead, so they didn't even notice their absence. I hadn't seen it until just now. No Sun and no parasites, something struck me then, when I removed the coyote's parasite and I saw that it had come from the stars, the Sun was a star, something about no stars in the underworld was on the tip of my tongue, but I didn't understand. Maybe the reason we could do anything in the lu-cidity of dreams was due to their absence. Perhaps the only moments of clarity, the only freedom from the parasites that people were truly able to get was in their dreams. I saw the dreary eyes of the people on the stairs. Maybe I can wake them up a bit, I thought to myself. I hov-ered off the ground. If Asher could do it, so could I.

Look! I shouted into their minds, *We are here, we can do whatever we want!! There is no reason for you to walk on the stairs! Fly! You are dreaming!!* I commanded them. I levitated, going up and down the stairs, trying so hard to get their attention trying to get them to notice.

Can't you see that I am doing something impossible? Can't you see that I am doing what is unimaginable? You can do it too! Do some-thing impossible with me! I had no influence over them at all. They looked upset that I had spoken so loudly in the library and weren't even listening to what I said. I looked around at the others and I could tell they had no clue. They were fast asleep. It was all I could do to refrain myself from judging them for their stupidity, but that's the thing about being stupid I guess, you don't know you are stupid, I had been there also.

I was so irritated but felt my awareness being drained by them, so I gave up and decided to look around instead. What could I do in the library I wondered, what does one do in a dream library, what was even in here? My mind must have brought me here for a reason. I went to the shelves and began glancing at the books. There were no titles on any of the books, they all had blank spines. I pulled out one of the leather bound older tomes and as soon as I lifted it free from its slot, the book transformed into the same bible from the motel room. Startled, I could feel my lucidity fading as I fell back into the lullaby of intrigue. I had summoned the bible before on purpose, circling ambiently, but now it was showing up on its own, it made me feel out of control and my confidence slipped. I placed it slowly back on the shelf trying to pay extra close attention, like watching a magician perform a trick. The book faded back into a nameless volume along with all the others. I walked, purposefully now, several more steps, stopped and pried another random book loose from the location like a dentist pulling a tooth. The second it emerged, it was the bible again. I stood there, staring at the bible laying in my hands, afraid to open it. I could see the place where my fingernails had scratched through the shitty pleather cover, and it had my blood on the pages from my papercut. Dammit, it has me again, the pull, I was hooked, I had to know what was in the book and I wanted to open it and look inside so badly, but part of me also knew that all that was in there was a can of worms. It was Pandora's box urging me to release it and be consumed. I thought I was choosing the path now, but what if there were no other options, what if all my choices were always rigged to return me back to where the mega dreamer wanted me to go?

I withheld my impulse to look in the book, although it took everything in me to do so. I put it back onto the shelf and as it mingled back into the illusion, a giant hand materialized from a black hole in the ceiling above me. Is this for real? It was eerily similar to Asher's appearance into my life. I was still in a dream, it was so beyond ridiculous that I rose back up into lucidity. The enormous hand settled on the ground before me with its palm up. I could sense its intention and it wanted me to stand on it, to mount it like a horse. I felt like I had passed some kind of test and made it in through a back door by refusing to play the bible game anymore. Maybe choosing not to choose was the only way to shift the path. There was finally some kind of force that was helping me and not trying to ruin my every move on the chess board. I hopped on the hand. I looked closely at it and could see the lines and patterns on its skin, it seemed like a topography map I had seen as a child. I was lifted up and moved through the library, riding along with it. I had spent so much time flying in dreams now, I wasn't used to something helping me and had gotten to like the feeling of having so much control and independence in the lucid state. Apart from the coyote helping me, I hadn't ever felt like the world was trying to help me, there was always some kind of obstacle I was working against or trying to go around. I tried to gaze up and see what the appendage was connected to, but everything got really blurry and just kind of faded away, I couldn't make anything out.

The hand laid me down in front of a shelf that was further back than all the rest, it was covered in cobwebs and spiders. I got a flash in my memory of the spider wife and fell into distrust for a moment before I took a deep breath trying to separate my memories from what was before me now, it was really hard to do. I was trying to go with the flow, but everything that had already happened kept fucking me up and disjointing me. I was still in Jake's body, the corpse, everything was a strange stream of half formed dreams. I had to press through the fog and continue. The mysterious hand retreated somewhere into the ceiling, leaving me there in the dusty dank corner. There was a faint light coming off the bookshelf so I went closer, despite the spiders, which now sent a special kind of shiver up my spine. One book was slightly askew, balanced precariously off the edge unnaturally. I had to suppress the feeling that this was some other test I was supposed to ignore and not engage in, because it felt different, it felt calm, I didn't have that same dreadful need to find something out, instead it was as though I was being guided by something to move forward. Like a friend would. I felt curious and filled with wonder.

I reached out my hand and grasped the book, it felt smooth and cool to my touch. I closed my eyes and snorted because I knew that I was closing my eyes within a dream, I had a brief schism as the thought entered me that I could keep closing my eyes forever in this way, closing my eyes was like a portal that placed me in another place where I could close my eyes again and then again and again. I shook my head to come back out of it and into the dream, the thought of the eternal blinking in and out of place threatened to carry me into outer space somehow, far far away. I opened my eyes and stared at the book, afraid that if I opened it I would only find the same bible again in some kind of cosmic prank. Was I supposed to resist looking, or was I meant to look? Some decisions were really hard to make when you had been tricked before.

I carefully felt the sides of the pages with my fingers and took a wild guess as to where the middle might be and braced myself as I threw open the book in my palm. There was not a bible before me, I couldn't even understand what I was seeing but I was grateful I hadn't just returned to the goddamn bible again. The circles were making me sick. What I was looking at wasn't a book at all, it was more like a movie screen. There was a scene playing over the pages of a green grassy meadow with a blue sky and puffy clouds floating by. It was beautiful. I looked closely and the meadow was familiar, there were white flowers growing everywhere . . . asphodels. It was the same meadow I had woken up from with Asher. A feeling crept over me like a spider crawling over my skin and I looked closer at the moving image. There was something about this place, as I was looking deeply into the picture, while remembering when I had been there, the smell, the feeling of it, a wave of vibration struck through my memory. This was another dimension, my mind thought to itself. It felt like a familiar person. I know it was a place, but it had a sense to it that was more like a relative or something, I couldn't even describe it. I pierced into it to try and discern what it was that I was picking up, it was the place, the location, I could feel it. The location had an identity, just like a person. The way I was feeling about this scene was as though I was looking through a family album. This place was a living thing, just like me. What was it though? As I wondered I got the feeling again of the thing that was dreaming me, I had crossed some threshold, it wanted me to remember it, it wanted to be remembered, here like this, that's why I had been brought to this long forgotten book. Why would the mega dreamer want me to remember this? I instinctively turned to ask the coyote and realized he wasn't there, where did he go? I needed to share this with someone, I wanted someone there with me. I thought his name in my mind, I was like; "*Come to me, coyote.*"

He barged in through the doors with dramatic panache and looked around. We locked eyes. No one seemed to even notice except for us, the only ones in on an inside joke while the rest of the world slumbered. They were like puppets on a stage going through the motions of their performance, what a strange existence for them.

Didn't I tell you I'm psychic? He said, smirking. Relief washed over me that he was there, the fact that he answered my call gave me total confidence, even though no one else seemed to even see me. I tucked the book into the back of my pants because I wanted to take it with me and I mounted into flight. I floated up in the air, it was as easy as breathing.

Let's get out of here. I motioned out the window. He grabbed me by my ankles and tried to pull me down, refusing to fly with me. He was yanking at me aggressively and I got pissed.

What is your problem? I thought, confused. I didn't care though, I kept trying to show off to the others, who were looking at us now, finally. I wanted to make them see something so jarring it would rouse them from their slumber. Whatever, I thought to myself. I can do anything so I just flew higher up and took him with me. I rose up in the building with the coyote dangling around my ankles, he was refusing to let go. I glanced at him and he seemed ridiculous, like a little kid being pulled into the sky holding onto a balloon. I looked down at him and thought;

Why aren't you flying too? I asked him.

You need to stay close to the ground. He answered.

Why? I retorted, feeling powerful and sick of people always telling me what to do.

Just listen to me, we both know things, remember? Reluctantly I descended back towards the ground. We looked around and both saw the door at the same time. He walked over to it motioning with his mind for me to follow. We poured out onto the street. There were people everywhere, it was so crowded we had trouble moving.

Ugh, I'm so bored, come on just a little bit, I said as I grabbed him by the back of his shirt and hovered slightly above the ground.

You are just going to draw the attention of the dreamer, they are going to feel you if you act differently and the world will turn on you to get you back to sleep. The coyote explained.

What? How did you know that? I hadn't thought he could figure something out that I couldn't and I felt myself getting jealous.

Look, I'm not a square, I have done plenty of sketchy shit in my day and if there is one thing I have learned, it's that sometimes it's better to go unnoticed. Don't you feel like something is watching us? I keep getting the creeps that something is there with me in this place. He was totally right. I was impatient though.

Fine, we will just go over their heads so that they can't see us. I reasoned. I positioned myself in the air over them like I was riding a hoverboard with my knees bent and indicated for him to do the same. Reluctantly, he followed my lead but I could tell he felt like we were about to get busted. We began riding the air like we were surfing, we couldn't help but smile. It was so cool. We were zooming through the streets just out of sight passing through the crowded city. People were going about their business below us and we were in on a joke together, living above the rules. Suddenly the scenery changed and the buildings turned into dirt. We were surfing through a canyon, all the people were still there. The people were wiggling in weird ways and something was up. We were caught in the dream web.

Shit. I told you so. Coyote said, proving himself right, we had been discovered. The people shifted and turned into marching soldiers made of dirt and clay, they were following us. Their faces all turned their gaze to us simultaneously in creepy unison. They couldn't fly though, I found that fascinating, if these were the soldiers of the dream realm, they sure were boring. They were stuck on the ground, in the dirt. I looked closer at them and it was clear they were made out of mud and part of the Earth they were walking on, almost fused into the ground, but still able to move. They were more like rolling over the ground, in unison, as I looked down on them from above they were like a centipede with strange puppet strings connecting them to the soil. Their faces were chiseled like statues and their expressions didn't change, which made them all the more terrifying. Coyote swiftly grabbed me by my sleeve and pulled me up out of the canyon to circle back around into the city again down a street.

In here, he said, pointing down an alleyway that was less crowded. There was a car on the road, it looked like a Rolls Royce. I had never seen one in real life, haha real life I caught myself.

Get in. I could sense that he was onto something but I was still trying to make it out, and a bit hesitant to let him lead. We got in the car. He took a moment and felt the car with his hands, enjoying it, I laughed to myself, oh, I got it. Totally made sense, it was his dream car. He pushed his foot all the way down on the gas and the tires were hugging the ground, he loved driving. I saw him drive like it was the first time. He loved to drive, it was his thing.

Look, see how fast we can go? he said. *This is safer, we have protection, like a suit of armor,* he assured me. I smiled and enjoyed watching him, he was a child but in a good way, I could see who he was. Even his sexual perversions were simple and basic. He was a simple kind of man who was what he was. I watched him and thought about all the times I was nervous to be myself, or upset that I wasn't something else. I doubted if he had ever felt that way.

A terrifying lightning storm broke into the sky. It came out of nowhere, striking all around us simultaneously. I was grateful for the car. The coyote was right, it was safer, we would have been torn to bits out there. Shit, it was no joke when nature decided to turn against you, even if it was dream nature. Hm, I thought, what is the difference between dream nature and real nature? I felt a feeling like when the hand had helped me. How could the outer world play such a role in our progress or demise through the guise of nature, it seemed so unfair. That was what power really was, big power anyway. I felt like the coyote's parasite must have when I overpowered it. Some things you had to submit to because you didn't have any choice, like a storm.

The voltage was connecting to the ground all around us. The coyote didn't stop, he sped up, he just kept going faster and faster, he could see exactly where he was going. I was still in the dark. He was steering around the strikes, determined and confident. A flashing bolt would fall and he would swerve, only to curve around another one. But we couldn't outrun them forever, even though he was a really good driver. A strike hit the car.

Don't touch the door, he said. *Keep your hands in your lap.* The whole car was throbbing with a bright blue light. I made sure I sat in the middle of my seat, with nothing touching the metal. I tried to suspend myself in mid air with a bumper of atmosphere between me and the world. While I floated there, I could feel a weird separation from this, from everything, I made a little pocket of time space where nothing was there but me. The coyote kept trying to explain his strategy to me.

The tires are rubber, it can't get us, the electricity can't get us here in the car. Just don't touch anything. He went faster and faster as the lightning kept piercing everything, I could feel the electrical charge on the car growing. More and more bolts were hitting the car, building the glow until it seemed as though we were riding inside of the Sun. I couldn't believe we were still driving.

Then we saw her. She was standing up ahead, eating . . . something, I couldn't tell what it was. He just kept driving, I got it, I could finally see what he was doing now. He didn't have to explain anything. We were riding along on a thought wave that didn't stop or interrupt with the annoying habit of talking. I felt free for the first time in my life. He could feel it too. It was the best feeling I had ever had. I remembered what Asher had said about being able to see everything like driving in a car looking at the mirrors. I could see the future like looking down the road. I held my breath. He pushed the gas as far down as it could go. We rammed into her going full speed with the entire gale following us. He had used the car to drag the storm, we were a mobile lightning rod. The car had been accumulating and attracting all the bolts, gathering the tempest into a solid shocking ball of mobile electric steel. She seemed to not understand what was happening or who we were. I saw a flash of her eyes as she tried to dislodge herself from her meal in the millisecond before we made impact.

Eat this, bitch. Coyote thought with a gleeful grin. The collision was instantaneous yet seemed to be in slow motion. It didn't cause the dull thud I expected, instead we had created a space inside of everything else, like the eye within a cyclone. A fold in time. The car came to a complete halt when it hit her, the blue light consumed the green glow, that was her, eclipsing it from existence. Time was suspended, I couldn't move. I felt the same way I had when the parasite was leaving me. It looked like she had been swallowed by a dragon, a big blue, electric dragon that was an interwoven mesh of crosshatched capillaries. The streams of voltage engulfed her entirely, wrapped her up in a plasma gown. When the lightning had devoured itself of its own accord, the coyote and I looked at each other wondering if it was safe to get out of the storm machine. We peered around, trying to make sure she wasn't hiding somewhere, and we made her even more powerful. Afraid the ground might be hot with residual charge, we didn't see anything, didn't feel anything. In fact, there was nothing there at all, just sizzling smoking steam crackling through the air. Cautiously, I opened the door, nothing. She had been totally annihilated, a pile of glittering green dust was scattered in the wind. The lightning had eaten her, they had fused together.

Well, I guess there goes our chance at reclaiming your body. the coyote said remorsefully. He had been looking forward to being a hero, I could feel his dismay.

Why not just grow a new one? I responded. Yes, it made total sense. Why can't I make another body for myself in here, I can do anything, after all. My body had germinated like a seed in the first place in some deep dark womb, why not just make it again like a starfish making another limb. If lizards could regenerate a tail, I should be able to re-capitulate my body. We were in the underworld, the same rules did not apply, there was no reason why I couldn't do whatever I thought. How fascinating that I kept forgetting the level of ability I had here, I kept having to chase down the memory of the opportunity available to me. I had flown, sprouted wings, but each instant that passed I kept shrinking back down to the same limitations I had in the over world. I had to constantly keep remembering here, had to keep reaching, keep shooting forth like those flowers I had seen in the field, what had Asher called them? Asphodels, I remembered. If I didn't keep constantly re-gathering everything in my mind, I would collapse back in upon myself into the small frail circle that contained me in the world above, the oppression, the restrictions, the regulations, the rules.

Grow a new one. I laughed to myself, "Grow a pair" the phrase everyone uses, I had to un-grow these balls. I had to farm myself. Prune the tree, like my body was a vegetable.

My body. I thought it out loud and the coyote seemed to understand as soon as I saw the knowing, the belief in his eyes that swelled with tears. I was able to feel as though it were true that I could create a new me. My figure already contained how to do it, what to do, I didn't need to do anything at all. My unconscious mind was an ocean vast and infinite. It wasn't my body and all bodies were kind of the same even in their differences. My unconscious was the key. I thought again. I rested there in that seat for a moment, thinking of what Asher had said. I am not my physique, I had been thinking of my body as separate from myself. Oh no. Asher had used my form on purpose. Not for him, but for me. I can't believe I hadn't seen it before. I am so stupid. My body did know, it did remember things I had forgotten, it could perceive things that I didn't, I had to come back into my body, into the memory palace that was my flesh. Any body though really, all bodies. All forms. I finally appreciated the flesh as something that was not me, was not my identity but was a wisdom palace that belonged to a bigger thing and that was part of me also. Like the dream belonged to a larger dreamer, it was the same thing. A body was a sack of materialized memories passed down through generations, waiting to be remembered, just as Asher had been waiting to be heard, to be free. It really wasn't about what my body had to do with me and who I was, it was about what was enfolded into it that I could access. That had nothing to do with me, but was still part of my experience, and something I could do.

I descended into my abdomen, but now it was more agitated, the same feeling that Asher had inspired. It was unfurling, more demanding now. I did not resist this time, did not try to shove it back down into me, out of fear. Instead I had a new feeling about it; curiosity. What is this, what would happen, what was going to come next? I couldn't help myself and my need to know overwhelmed the feeling of fear. One feeling subsumed the other until the fear receded into the background and I followed the new action un-withheld, uninhibited.

I tried to chase down the source of it, the place where it was coming from, the muscles, the nerves, the bones. No one ever feels their bones, I thought to myself. The marrow of my memories was like a vast structure of scaffold bones within some kind of matrixed marble. I sank into the quicksand of what it was in there. The second I made the connection, a pulse of light emitted from it and I shed the body of Jake like a husk, I could see it, like a mannequin there, on the floor as I levitated. An eggshell of an exterior. Coyote was staring at me, but his face wasn't his, I could see something else. I could see . . . him, inside himself, the flesh was just some kind of appendage like a puppet that someone else was driving from inside, I could see him now, like a child. He had one of him inside his body too, a thing that never changed. A thing that was eternal, an egg. I fell back to the ground then and the pulse stretched more rhythmic, going in and out, each time it pulsed a wave emitted growing fascia, forming bones extending veins and sinew. Contracting, expanding, contracting expanding.

My body was unfolding like a tree in sped up time. It was growing out of that eternal place somewhere in my belly. I had always thought the mother created the body but this was not true. All the mother did was hold the space, provide nourishment. It was the true self, the inner self where our body fattened, a tree from an acorn, from the inside out. I kept pulsing and thrashing about. Coyote was kneeling wisely at my side, waiting and patient, he too witnessed what was happening, just an understanding of the truth of an unfolding event that was self-evident and observable.

I rocked in fits, gasping air into my new lungs and pounded the ground with my new palms, and then it was over. Everything was calm and still. I opened my eyes. Coyote was looking at me, smiling, I was Angela again. I did it. I had done it. I sat up looking around. We were still in the underworld, but I had retrieved myself. I found my way back from the inside out. I was just me, I could feel my me-ness and it surrounded me in soothing serenades. We looked over at Jake's corpse and I felt so sad for him. I wondered where his egg had gone. It had to be somewhere. I thought it was wrong to just leave him there like that. So much had happened to me inside of him. The coyote felt me and my concern but didn't seem to share my care for Jake.

Should we bury him, you think? He asked, trying to be polite, but very excited that I was Angela again.

Ok, I guess there isn't much else we can do. I wasn't really sure how you bury something in the underworld, I thought the underworld was where the dead go anyway, what happens when the dead die in the underworld? I guess it's like a zombie dying again or something, I was forgetting all the horror movie rules. We started pulling our hands through the dirt, digging our fingernails into the soil to move enough of it to make him a bed.

It's like he can go to sleep now, maybe he will have a nice dream some-where, link up with the big dreamer maybe? I said.

I never thought of that before, the coyote's mind became philo-sophical. *I guess that's kind of what happens when we die too, we just turn back into the Earth, that must be who is dreaming all of us right? Maybe he will turn back into a dream.*

Maybe. Coyote was right, it was the Earth, that's who the mega-dreamer was, I couldn't believe I had been so stupid, this was about the Earth, the whole time. We had cleared enough space to drag his body in and laid him carefully in, folding his arms neatly over his chest. I began undressing him because he was wearing Angela's clothes and I decided to put them on my new old body, to the coyote's dismay. I no-ticed something sticking out of the back of Jake's pants as I took them off and reached down to see what it was. It was the strange book I had been taken to in the library, I had forgotten all about it. As soon as my hand grasped it, the fragrant Earth surrounding Jake's husk seemed to come to life and moved itself over him. I heeded its intentions and was taken aback as the inside of my mind unfolded. I placed the book, open to the middle, on top of the grave, the coyote was seeing it for the

first time and stood enraptured by it, looking at the animated image of
the field of asphodels. Burial was like planting flowers, I mused to myself, maybe we were like flowers when we die, planted to sprout again.
We gazed into it as the living soil settled into place and I had the same
feeling of familiarity, like this place too was like the same meadow. The
coyote could observe where my mind was traveling and he knew we
were dancing on the edge of something.

How are we going to make the bridge Angela? Coyote asked me calmly, it wasn't as though he needed an answer, it was more like he was
guiding me to the next step, because his vision saw we would do it.

*We just need to remember it, my friend, it's already there. Hey,
what's your first memory, the first thing in your life you can remember?*
I asked him playfully.

Jeez, I don't know, let me think about it. He paused and his eyes were
searching for it, like it was visible. How interesting, I thought, that our
eyes move when we remember, just like the rapid eye movement of a
dream.

Yes, you will need to think when you want to remember. I thought-
spoke. We must think to remember, like hunting, it's like chasing after
an animal, until you catch sight of its tail, and then once you lock onto
it, you catch it, the whole thing comes forth. It emerges, where before
it wasn't. Your mind can be blank and then suddenly fill with everything from your memory like a waterfall.

"Ever have a dream you couldn't remember and then someone says
something during the day and it reminds you of what someone said
in the dream and then the whole thing explodes into your mind, like
fireworks?" I said out loud, using my voice for the first time in a while.

"Hey, that reminds me," He was talking too now. "The first thing
I can remember, it hit me, I was at the park with my parents. It was a
beautiful day, I was laughing. I looked up and I saw a dog across the
park. I loved dogs and I got up to run over to it. I heard my mother
yell my name but I didn't listen to her, I just recall pain and darkness
and confusion. It was so intense and so abrupt. I had gotten kicked in

the head by a kid on a swing. It wasn't their fault of course, I walked into it. But I recollect it so clearly now. I wonder why I remember that moment more than any other," he pondered to himself.

"Because of the pain," I answered flatly. "That's what Asher said anyway," I stated, to make sure he knew it wasn't my observation and to give Asher honor and remembrance.

"That is your first memory, but that isn't the first thing that happened to you," I elucidated. "Can you imagine trying to remember your first memory of your existence? That's a crazy thought, right? The first thing that happened, that you can't remember, was that you were grown from a seed. And before that, the seed had come from somewhere. We came from somewhere, we can close the circle. That's how we make the bridge," I said encouragingly. I picked up the magic book with the living meadow and closed it. I opened it again and it was the bible. I turned to the page with the ashes of Asher on it, on the psalm proclaiming enduring love and took some between my fingertips. I placed the ashes on my tongue in an autophagous act of communion.

"A circle is a snake that eats its tail, self-consuming no beginning and no end, it is only a middle," I stated, like some tape loop were playing from out of my mouth, out of somewhere that wasn't me. The ashes descended through me tearing into my tissues. My middle, my center. They sat there for a moment, heavy as a brick.

Did you know you also have a brain in your stomach? I asked the coyote through my belly. *They say it's older than your mind brain.* I laughed, mind brain. The ash is the seed and we may return to it.

That is where I am speaking to you from now. Memory is the bridge. Memory is the bridge. But not our memory. The evocation of a time much older than us, we are here to remind it of something but I'm not sure what yet. Even as we talk, right now it is trying to come forth trying to crest on a wave that swells up from somewhere, some location where it is waiting, folded in, it is pacing back and forth now, can you feel it? He closed his eyes. We drifted into the feeling together, trying to stoke a reminiscence.

If I make my memory of what is above and what is below come together, I can bridge the upper and lower worlds. Its mind, its memory, it isn't a location, the location is mind itself!

The red grid appeared around us as everything else faded away.

Look there, I motioned for him to gaze with his eyes at the pulsing red light. We stared at it together. The closer I looked, I discerned the light, there were lines coming out of it, rays emanating out of each line of the grid, it was lines made out of lines extending into lines. We looked closer, trying not to blink. The lines looked like veins or rivers. They were branching off of each other into complex fractals. They were all refracting off each other. They bubbled up and out into spheres.

What? Coyote implored, he could not believe his eyes.

Shh it's remembering, quiet. I thought. The bubbles accumulated, like red blood cells streaming together. It was, creating itself, as I had grown my body, the memory was causing it to grow. Maybe everything being created was just happening from some kind of larger memory, a rebirthing, that just kept repeating over and over again. It was a kind of cosmic ooze now, frothing and throbbing there before us, growing, it was . . . disgusting, the smell was burning tar. It was full of gargling orifices that were opening and stretching, lowly lichen reaching for the moon. Shapes were circulating throughout, sometimes faces or beasts, geometries and crystals, shooting forth and being swallowed back. A millennia of moments, magma gushing out. Overlapping ovals and membranes pushing through. We were completely entranced, like we ceased to exist, empty specters.

My body began to twitch, out of my control. The muscles could hear its memories, and were responding in sympathetic chords. The source, whatever it was, was pulling me, threads in my skin were separating, being tugged out of me. The coyote's body was responding too, I could see it, I could feel it. He looked scared, I saw the panic on his face. It was going to overwhelm us, devour us into itself. We were going to lose our bodies in it as they begged to be returned to their mother. Filled with fear at its power, old and strong and beyond my control my brain was a frantic, static scream.

"No!" I commanded confidently, just as I had to the gatekeeper when it had encroached upon me, I lunged my hand to join with the coyote's and repeated, "No!" It was like throwing rocks at a hurricane. There was nothing I could do, the thing was massively doubling every second. Coyote and I looked at each other. We were fucked.

"We have to get out of here," he said desperately.

"Yes we do," I answered. A memory raced through me like a car driving by. It was Jake's memory, or when I was still Jake rather, when I was attacked by the spider wife and I showed it to the coyote, as though I was making him watch a show. It took less time than trying to speak and explain it to him. He looked at me indicating he understood what to do. It was worth a try.

"On the count of three, blink as hard as you can while looking at it. Ready?"

"Ready."

"1 . . . 2 . . . 3!" We closed our eyes hard, blinked, and then we were somewhere else, somewhen else. The zoetrope had turned, the merry-go-round spun on an axis. We were in the overworld. But it was also the underworld. Shit. I could still see the red grid, it was there permeating everything now. Was I dreaming this? Maybe this was a trick and we were going to wake up. I looked down, I had Angela's body, so I knew I had made some kind of progress, or had I gone somewhere before anything happened? It was hard to tell. The worlds were superimposed upon each other in an overlay, it appeared like when I had been looking out the window of the motel room on the wet rainy streets. We had been transported, but where we had been came with us as though it was attached to our feet. But it wasn't on our feet, it was linked onto our minds. We had brought it through. Somehow it had used our memory as its pathway. The passage was complete. Oh no, the bridge was complete. I hadn't stopped to think about what that would mean. I didn't understand it meant I was going to be bringing this kraken back with us! The marriage of the over and underworld was taking place before us and we were filled with an existential dread. I couldn't stop it. We looked at each other. Coyote realized it too. I had just made a bridge for that ancient thing to cross.

Parthenogenesis

We relocated through the dimensions into the middle of a city. I could feel everything. The wind was the first thing I saw, strange, I thought, you can't see the wind, you feel it. But I *saw* it pouring over me, the air was a river, flowing over my skin. I'm swimming, I thought. The sky is an ocean. I couldn't tell the difference between feeling and seeing anymore, they had been smooshed together in a big sticky mess. The sidewalk shifted under our feet as I watched the buildings heave a sigh. I was certain I imagined an earthquake might be coming, the ground was liquifying. All my hairs stood up, expectant for anything. Coyote was just trying to watch everything, ready for what might happen. I lowered my gaze and saw I was holding the bible, I didn't remember grabbing it and felt creepy that it was there with us. I dropped it on the ground with a thud and it opened, splitting in two. I could see it had cracked right to the center again. Everything slowed down, exaggerated and surreal, I looked at my feet, the ground was shaking. Not natural, something different. I heard snapping sounds as the streets cracked. Something crept in beside me, I saw paws, big black paws. An enormous black panther stood with us, standing steady even though the Earth shook, it was not moving, it was the only thing that was still.

It was him, I knew his mind anywhere. I felt in my bones that this panther was Asher. Asher was here with us, the singed tiger, turned to ally. Asher had been released from the bible again here in the overworld, resurrected. Maybe nothing died in the underworld, like it was a practice space or something where there weren't any consequences. I hoped that portion of it would be brought here now. The panther had bright red eyes that looked like blood. We stared into each other and I felt calm amidst the chaos. I had been there to serve the creature and not the other way around. I was the ally of the panther, it did not belong to me. Asher was here now and knew that its mission had been accomplished. Asher was able to return across the bridge I made, return from the underworld, from the land of the dead. It was me, after everything was said and done, I was the bomb Asher had wanted all along. I did it because I made it about me, Asher knew this, tried to tell me, I just wouldn't listen. I would betray them for my own power and now, I had done it myself, instead of just following Asher's commands. Here, after incineration, Asher had returned, the jaguar, product of the trial by fire. I guess it didn't matter now, because the task was completed. The worlds were united, the change initiated and there was no stopping it. I traveled into the panther's red gleaming eyes and connected to its ancient sentience.

It is good, do not be afraid. The voice pierced into me. The coyote reeled, he heard it too, and knew everything. As the understanding coursed into the coyote, I could sense him going through so many feelings at once, betrayal, regret, grief, impotence.

All will change now. As is meant to be. For the greater. The words were a spooky prophecy and all we could do was watch what happened next, I certainly knew Asher wouldn't be answering any questions. The pavement was dissolving like salt in water. The Earth erupted, draining out all over the city. The soil surfaced, bleeding into civilization, through the concrete cage. Then the worms came. They were frenzied, attempting to escape. Nowhere to go but into each other, they formed huge writhing masses. Desperate waves unifying in undulation. An orgy of serpents, a holographic Leviathan. Millions making one. Expelled and exposed, the soil kept rising, pushed from below, underneath. The sweat dropped into my eyes. It was getting hot. Muggy through the fog, I could barely see. Hot damp earth moving, an ancient jungle was reclaiming the territory from below. Coyote was sweating too, the panther was calm and unmoving.

Out of the frying pan. Coyote thought into me, making sure he was right beside me no matter what might happen.

Walk through the fire. The panther's answer. The surrounding sweltering mist mingled with my own sweat pouring down my face. Fog is Earth sweat, I laughed to myself. I am you, Earth, I see so clearly. Tropical warmth inside the lungs of some creature. The Asher panther wasn't sweating, even though it was covered in fur. The worms were trying not to be cooked alive. Had to start to move my feet, if I stood in one place too long my shoes would smoke. I set out walking but I didn't know where, every street the same thing was happening. Desperate worms silently screaming in morbid dances. Sulfur hit my nose and punched my face. I heard coyote gag. Tears streamed down my cheeks that crystallized into sleeping sand the second they touched my skin. Soon my face was encrusted with a mask like a bandit, salty sunglasses I could not see through. I scraped my cheeks with my fingernails, it hurt. I tore off a piece of my shirt and tied it as a blindfold, I could see better that way even though my eyes were closed.

I don't need my eyes, I thought to myself and the coyote simultaneously. He was going through the same thing.

We can do what we want here too, we can do it here too. I kept repeating, trying to remember the feeling. I could fly here too, I thought. I am lucid here too, I thought. I strained my memory, reaching for the feeling. Yellow flames flashed thick smoke, fire dancing sunbeams through the blinds. Hypnotized for a moment I stood sweating, crying crusty tears among the crystal rain. I could feel the coyote next to me. I saw by understanding. I saw by feeling. The pores of my skin opened, an audience of eyes. Asher was unaffected, simply standing, watching through its panther gaze. Thunder filled my ears till I thought they would break. My belly ached and hurled. The pulse, the memory, BOOM, my eyes pulsed, BOOM, it shot through my hands and feet.

I stopped and stood still in a statue pose. I searched with my mind. Eyes closed. To see if I could feel. I forgot about my eyes. The edge of my skin was taught as a drum against the air. Then I went beyond its boundary until everything disintegrated. I went past myself into space, feeling the emptiness. My mind brushed it, sensitive like a whisker. I could feel Asher's whiskers. My body rippled, taking it in. My blood threatened to lurch out of my body into the cosmos, pushing from inside of me, I was burning like the worms. I saw it, I saw what was happening then. I could feel the coyote next to me feeling it too. Not only was I lucid now, but everything was, everything. All things were fully aware. The dirt, the ground, the air, everything was waking up. Oh God, how could I think this would just be people? How could I think it would just be me? The enmeshment of life, of the organism, of the Earth relayed back and forth through me in its chthonic reality. Everything was waking up, not just me. Not just me.

"Shit!" I said out loud.

"Run!" he said.

We came running around the corner, a girl, a panther and a coyote. Echoes of what we left behind faded into the distance, made into mountains of memory. The gaze of our mind's eyes turned to the surroundings. The ground under my feet was wriggling and writhing as if it were a cartoon. I swept the scene before me and took in the extent of the escalating reverberations. Just as I had been able to discern Asher's mind, I could sense another here, now. There was something all around us, something familiar. It was that thing that spoke to me when I felt it dreaming me. It was here now. The mega dreamer. The being I was inside of, we were all inside of. It had made itself known to me and now I recognized it was here. I felt like I was being watched by something I could not see. There was no running away from this, it would be like trying to outrun your own feet, impossible. It was, the

Earth. We were on it, in it and of it and there was nothing to do now but welcome it.

I felt Asher the panther next to me and had a convergence of thoughts. The intersection of lines all rejoined circling back. Asher was the servant of this thing. I was just reflecting something Asher was to it, a mirror with a thousand faces. I helped Asher, Asher helped the mega dreamer. Everything came from somewhere, all the locations, all the memories, everything I had mapped. Where was it from? This was the first time I ever had that question enter my awareness. I knew they were there and had figured out they made circles and could even pinpoint the center. But how did something exist? I can't believe I was so stupid. I made my body, but only because I already had it before. Where did it come from? Where did I come from? I screamed within myself and everything sucked into the center of a black hole. The thing that we brought through was the thing that was dreaming me, it was the thing that created me. It was the source of dreams themselves. It was the dream giver, the mega dreamer. I broke free from my self delusion and could see everything so clearly.

It was not just the ground, but the trees, the sky, the buildings all were moving and undulating to some rhythm far beyond my senses. Shockwaves pulsing like everything had just turned into liquid. I turned to him to make sure I wasn't insane and as his mind met mine, the madness was not my own. His mouth was open in disbelief and neither of us said a word. I knelt down and placed my hand on the Earth to try to pop out of the hallucination but all I felt was a greater un-ease. The Earth itself was moving, contracting from somewhere deep within. I drew closer to feel insects crawling out of the mud. Was it Bugs? My mind could see but it was blurry night vision goggles.

"What is that?" he said, my thoughts took flight through his words as he asked what we were trying to fathom

"It feels like . . ." Before I could respond, the balls of dirt gathered together in clumps and those drew in others, amassing into millions of vortex points all around us. It was not bugs. It was the Earth herself, sentiently convulsing into shapes.

"Run!" I heard coyote say before I could decipher what was happening, he slipped his hand roughly into mine and dragged me to a spot of cement. I could sense Asher laughing in his mind at our efforts. The panther followed in our footsteps as if in jest to our alert. We tried to run but the ground gave way beneath our feet like we were walking through powdered snow. The patch of concrete was the only thing unaffected by the swirling mass of transformational chaos spilling out of the elements before us. The muddy mess was much larger than insects now, grown to the size of rats. They had taken on an animalistic appearance in the few minutes we had been absorbed by moving our bodies out of their midst. The creatures were being created simultaneously in the earth, wind and water everywhere. All we could do was watch, powerless from our perch as the world changed into the spirit of the living things that drove all of its forces. The elements were concentrating into life forms. The Earth beings heaved into themselves with shuddering trembling force as each one took the shape of its Deva. Long slumbering forces have been awakened, now rising up into birth and faeries participating in some parthenogenetic dance of arousal spewing them out of every available material.

The entities precipitated from the skies overhead as well as underfoot and we both looked over beside us as we heard a loud and sickening thud, whose source was terribly revealed as a hapless cloud being had learned the unforgiving slap of gravity. Asher placed a paw upon it to keep it still. We bent down to view the incredible expression of energetic amalgamation. The being was like some kind of sea slug that had sprouted wings, perhaps this one had fledged too quickly and not gained use of its flimsy, etheric wings before the fist of the Earth dragged it down to its doom. Iridescent rainbow colors caught the light on its radiating appendages still and limp at our feet. We turned up towards the Heavens to see thousands of them dripping out of the expanse of the horizon like hordes of locusts. Some of them rammed into each other in their desperate pursuit of escaping the ground and as they collided, their bodily blobs united with each other, transmuting into larger creatures, serpents stretching out till dragons filled the spaces between the smaller slimy grubs.

The trees were disassembling themselves. The bark was crying tears of sap from every crevice that sprang out into honey octagons that mixed with the frantic earth creatures under them, creating appendages over the mud beings that took on the likeness of spun silk. The sap sunk into their backs in spines of blood and those poor beasts moaned as their shapes changed yet again into shining reptilian giants that proceeded to feed upon the scurrying soil fairies.

"Everything is evolving simultaneously in each second that passes," I vaguely heard myself muttering amidst the din of noise that was amplifying into a buzzing shrieking plague that filled the air. I removed my eye covering and opened my eyes again, scraping the sand off of them. The particles fell into the soil making a glass menagerie as if the sand knew what it had been before, a memory play. My crystalized tears grew into flowers that morphed into birds and flew off into the sky.

"Yes, nature is having an orgy with itself," he said as we looked into each other's eyes in a deep understanding of the unfolding process that was no longer reversible. I saw some of his hair escape his head and crawl down his back like a serpent.

"What do we do?" I asked him, trying to cover the fear in my shaking voice that could barely catch its breath. We both watched as one of my fingernails shivered its way off my hand, taking the form of a beetle that scuttled off into the fray.

"We can only change ourselves," he said, his voice was dark and low and full of truth. "There is nothing we can do to alter this," he said. We sat motionless staring at the life force for what seemed an eternity, I think I stopped breathing. Things continued to get much worse. The animated elemental creatures were all waging war with each other in vicious attempts to survive. The tree varmints were devouring as much earth animals as they could pour into them that promptly spilled out of them lifeless, only to rearrange into new life forms that collided again into bigger beasts that were overtaking the trees. The sky dragons were burning everything, shooting hot streams of smoke and steam onto anything that came across their path. Some of the larger dragons had morphed into each other making humongous storm creatures that shot lightning and thunder out of their mouths in angry gaping shouts. I watched as one of them crashed and fell into the earth leaking Lava that burbled up from below and swallowed the storm into itself swirling up and hardening into sharp spikes, obsidian shards that darted across the firmament.

"What have we done?" I whispered.

"Don't look," he said. I looked into his eyes and tried to concentrate. Coyote looked at me like I was very far away. I can't remember how long I had stopped breathing. I just went still. I closed my eyes but I could see everything. I saw him in front of me, looking back. He had an outline of faint blue light that pierced out in golden streaks. Behind him, in a majestic array I could see them, all of them. I relaxed my face and settled into my breath drawing in acceptance and trying to release my resistance to this new reality. The living, lucid things. I wasn't scared anymore because they were just as they should be. I didn't need to understand what was happening anymore. Asher gave me a silent nod in his mind, supporting my realization. All I had to do was keep on breathing. Coyote's fingers grazed my cheek as he had the same epiphany and we mysteriously understood exactly what to do while Asher sat calmly. I could see Asher's paws turning into trees that were rooting down into the soil. Its feet were stretching out into wooden creepers that were like vines, sprawling across and through the ground. Coyote grabbed my hands in his as we turned to face the new world. Everything was different now. Everywhere I looked I saw things evolve the moment my line of sight locked in, nothing was as it had been the moment before. I noticed there was a smallish lump of clay that had become predatory and cruel. The longer I held my eyes upon it, the shape of it convulsed, erupting in bursts and sprouts of growth.

I briefly turned away and saw that he was looking at the same one, I could see streams of light pouring from his face in the direction of the Earth entity. Just then there was a tug at my leg. My eyes jerked down to the source, The clay, it was almost human now, smallish and crude but humanoid. It had stolen our shape through our interaction and was mirroring it back to us in its evolution in some distorted pantomime. Its small hand grasped my leg and was urging my attention. My eyes poured into its visage and I saw it take on my features. Its face was growing out of itself, emerging into crystallization I retreated my attention back to coyote and the creature emitted a sound, begging for my adulation once more, I could feel its need for my gaze in order to remain feeding off my attention.

"We can't look at them," I said to him, breaking the hypnotic heavy haze that had enraptured us for a moment.

"But they are everywhere!" he yelled back at me in defiant observation.

"When we look at them they become us," I said quite plainly. All things were trying to evolve, even us, but this need to evolve was coming from somewhere else, it was coming from the mega dreamer, from the Earth itself as a creature. These forms wanted our attention because it gave a precious commodity, awareness, lucidity. We had Lucidity now and we could spread it anywhere we focused our minds. They wanted our consciousness.

"Just look at the Sun!" I retorted. I ignored the protests of the muddish dwarf and set my mind upon the blazing disk as it drew nearer to the horizon. The Sun was what was missing in the underworld so maybe if we gave our attention to it we could amplify the overworld. I knew now the reason there was no Sun in the underworld was because it was hidden by the night itself, the Earth's shadow, the Earth's dream. I could feel him adjusting his intent toward the light that was starting to sprawl through the dragon strewn sky. Daynight was coming, I could see the dark blue seeping in above us as the depths of space precipitated. I didn't know what would happen if the Sun disappeared behind the Earth's shadow, what would happen in the new night? The Sun was back now which meant the Earth must be moving again, so I just had to keep my gaze upon it.

"Stay still," he said slowly. I listened and felt into my feet, laying them squarely on our small portion of stability. A single square in a sea of frothing madness and monsters cresting at the shore. Everything looked pink, the consciousness of everything was solidifying and for a moment, I could have sworn, the world was a pale rose. Then it faded into hues of yellow and gold as I caught the shaft of Sun split the skyline as a sword, glinting in a sheen.

The Sun was inserting itself into everything. I closed my eyes and still I could see it. The slow syrupy light hit my face and I could feel it hot and warm. I couldn't hear the creatures any more. I focused on the light. It shone through my closed eyelids making everything blush. There was a small tap on my shoulder, he had shuffled his footing and rubbed against me, breaking the silence. I forgot about the Sun for a moment, he reached out and spread his fingers wide around my hand. His grip was joined by other fingers, cold and small. We both looked down and there were many of them. Little people, little clay people. There was a big one, the one we had been looking at, they had made it up onto our island and were staring at us, touching us. We jerked our hands away, breaking the connection and they complained like abandoned children.

"Just keep looking at the Sun!" I shouted angrily. He grunted and we both turned back towards the light. Everytime we placed the focus of our gaze upon the Sun, I noticed it chased away the cobwebs in my mind. The Sun was keeping the underworld from consuming everything. The difference between life and death was the Sun, it was the star that was the life provider. Without its gaze all went to sleep. Everything started to gather in my awareness like the folds of a skirt and I came into a moment of clarity. The sleep came with the darkness, when the light of the Sun wasn't there, when the Sun was shining, it could not set in, if only the Earth could always see the Sun, could be lit everywhere by its rays, be surrounded by its light, that was the key, the end to the darkness the end of night. The answer was the Sun. How could the light shine forth everywhere upon the Earth at once. No more intervals in darkness. Then and only then could the Earth and all its life enter into a sleepless day. I felt a rumble under my toes, as though the ground was responding to my thoughts, agreeing with me.

"Look at the Sun! Don't blink your eyes!" I yelled again. Coyote and I did not break our gaze, we kept vigilant like sentinels, staring and each second that we lasted we felt the darkness crawl away, it was disintegrated, as if by a laser beam. Something quickened and the Earth was symphonic in its response. As long as we do not close our eyes, we can do this, I thought.

"Keep going, don't stop!" I yelled. It was working and something peaked. The Earth was rising to the surface of her skin now, we had done it, crossed the threshold.

Asher was being swallowed up by the Earth that was erupting all around us and the hoards of mud men and our feet left the touchstone, floating into space.

We were flying. We hadn't even done it on purpose, it just kind of happened like it was natural. We were deathless, lifeless. Angela was a memory, a dream. I let everything go. To have power was as simple as taking a breath. How could death threaten? When there was breath. Coyote merged with me as our minds became one harmonious song. We/it/I/they began our ascent. Have to get high enough, we thought. Need to build up the force in order to go deep enough, we thought. We climbed and climbed, nothing but clouds now. Cold, we thought, though we didn't shiver. The light faded. Everything was getting darker. I could feel the world, the circle, a sphere that it was. I could see everything. I looked up and saw my mother, my true mother, where I came from. Beautiful, a vast void, no light within, but all light within. I looked at it, and my gaze enfolded it, all that had ever been in an instant. Felt all it had ever felt. Released all my flesh. This body I had fought so hard for meant nothing now. Even the Earth wasn't the real source of me, only my body came from the mega dreamer. As we made our way deeper into the stars I saw the source of the eggs, of the seeds, the self within me I had come to know. The seeds of us had been planted into the bodies of the Earth by something still bigger, something . . . something we couldn't quite reach.

The feeling of expansion filled everything, an infinite horizon. A never-ending fractal. Peace and calm filled everything, we could feel the pinnacle and stopped for a moment, still and free. We/it/I/they fell, swirling and spinning. Formless now, we shaped ourselves into a spear and made the descent. We fell quickly, and yet, motionless, still. I couldn't tell if we were moving or perfectly suspended. The Earth was foreign now, small now, different now, separate from us. We had to go back, to return in order to share with it all what we had seen/been/done and grown into. We/it/I/they were going to share a dream with the dream giver, after all it had given us, this was going to be wonderful. Our gift to this place. I remembered my Earth body, where I had been born, the place where it was to lay. An empty grave because my body had become a new being. No grave for me, I laughed. There was no longer an underworld to trap the dead, there would never be another tomb. We were pulled into a whirlpool as we approached, the tug was so strong, the enfolding arms of the Earth greeted us, we accepted our inevitable plunge deep within the heart of the soil we had originated from in the first place. We were going home. Not as a grave but as a womb. This would begin a new time for one and all. We were the medicine, our union would bring life to all, unite all things. We were the living death bringing birth within these caverns of the Earth. The ground rushed to meet us with its arms open wide. We could feel its love, its desire for us. We had been where it could not go and were returning to share the story. Relief filled me as we entered the humus, the human, the soil surrounding us, suffocating. I was wrapped up in vines that crept over me like a serpent, it was Asher. I was being integrated, coyote too. We were being made bigger through a disintegration. I sent my mind around and could sense that every creature that had ever lived was here also, stored within the soil. An archive of everything that ever existed, that had ever set foot on her was folded into the dirt, unified and screaming their stories. Fossils and bones, for her, were identical to my own memories. Songs, for the Earth, were played upon the ribs of one and all in underground symphonies. The recorded history of all of the Earth's existence lay here like a museum of life. I had always thought of the ground as a place for the dead, but what I realized was that it was a chronicle of carcasses, suspended within a matrix of memorials. Unbreathing monuments for all time. There was no more need for breath. The Earth drank us in, listened to us like a bedtime story. She trembled and expanded, shivering into what we had brought her. The conception was undeniable. As our minds entered her, she woke up, we had given her new seeds.

So it was created, the circle that was the Earth shifted its shape. All things come back around again but if the link is broken, if a step is taken, the circle becomes a spiral, a serpent, an undulating wave that can come free of its prison. A crack in the shell multiplied, as an egg shattering. A center point in its middle broke open and erupted into an expansion. The circle unfolded into a snake that released its tail. Emanating, contracting and releasing, the archetypal entity of a Dragon germinated from an infinity contained within the circle. Its form articulated and was made manifest. A Dragon, resplendent and crimson. An embodiment of ancient realization that was, the Earth. The Dragon spread its crystal wings in a thunder clap. I could feel everything, the stars whirling in the Heavens around me and the worms crawling within me. As I felt the waves of the celestial bodies hitting me, I saw them, I heard them, I smelled them. I was as a whale submerged, hearing and seeing the sonar of millions of songs through the waters. I am a living breathing massive creature that is the Earth. I am both within it and feeling from its perspective simultaneously. We had become one. She was in here with me. Coyote was here, I could feel him. Asher was here, and maybe had been a part of her already, I think I knew now that we all were. She moved us and started to fly, I would be with her always now. I had become her, but still myself. What was left of me within our belly decomposing into my new beingness freed from myself, from my seed to enter into a higher awareness, and even greater lucidity than I had ever imagined. Remnants of a vision I had been becoming, that had long been forgotten, something that had never existed before. A cosmic Earth being. The Sun would never be hidden from our view now, there was no more dreaming, no more darkness. We were surrounded by the pitch of space, lit up by all the stars who ceased their slumber long ago. It was our destiny to chase the stride of the Sun across outer space. This was the end of sunsets and sunrises. We soared into the new endless dawn of daynight as she spread our wings and we took to the abyss, shhh shhh shhh, the sound of her flight, spiraling the Sun through the Universe.

"The past and future dreams us, lies on our bodies like skin that we might pass the days with grace. To us were given all the ways and the obligation to travel. To us were opened all the roads of heaven, all the tunnels in earth and the channels of sea. Among the dead and the living, by these same words have we all traveled. Together we walk a single path into the heart of the infinite."

—— Normandi Ellis, *Awakening Osiris: A New Translation of the Egyptian Book of the Dead*

About the Author

Maja is a practicing witch and published scholar of alchemy and occult lore with an interest in the esoteric arts that spans her entire lifetime. After completing her bachelor's degree in Biochemistry, Maja studied Oriental Medicine and acupuncture, later receiving her master's degree in transformational psychology. Her master's thesis focused on Shamanism, the I Ching and ancestors. Maja was the librarian at the Philosophical Research Society, founded by Manly P. Hall, for eleven years, where she taught courses on Alchemy. Maja lectures occasionally on mysterious topics in Los Angeles.